CW00983725

Death in the Winter Garden

Antoine, a wedding photographer, goes missing during the photo-session at the Greyhavens Winter Garden of a wedding at which Superintendent Alan Mason and his wife happen to be guests. Later that night his premises are firebombed and someone spending the night there is asphyxiated. The portfolio of Antoine's photography proves to be of subjects more varied than weddings, and photography is not the extent of his business affairs. But who is Antoine? Who might bear him a grudge?

Sorting out the tangle is the responsibility of Superintendent Mason. Does the onlooker see more of the game, and does the camera never lie?

by the same author

FRANCIS LYALL

Death in the Winter Garden

THE CRIME CLUB
An Imprint of HarperCollins *Publishers*

First published in Great Britain in 1993
by The Crime Club, an imprint of
HarperCollins Publishers, 77–85 Fulham Palace Road,
Hammersmith, London W6 8JB

9 8 7 6 5 4 3 2 1

A catalogue record for this book is
available from the British Library

ISBN 0 00 232478 4

Photoset in Linotron Baskerville by
Rowland Phototypesetting Ltd
Bury St Edmunds, Suffolk
Printed and bound in Great Britain by
HarperCollins Book Manufacturing, Glasgow

CHAPTER 1

FRIDAY

Outside the Orangerie it was drizzling—a standard winter day. The gusty wind tugged at the few persistent leaves, and gathered and rearranged their less-determined fellows into brown, sodden drifts. The trees, bare to the weather, braced themselves for snows and frost to come while simultaneously gesturing to the sky, mutely praying for the spring.

Inside was a different world. It was warm and cheerful. The overhead lights had been turned on and the heating system was running. The plants were convinced they were in the tropics rather than in cold bleak Greyhavens. In the main greenhouse the budgies and parakeets were even beginning to explore next-boxes. They were the lucky ones. Saved from the certain death of the freedom they had rashly sought and freed by the police into this limited heaven, they swooped and chattered. Below them, beds of blue hyacinths interspersed with King Alfred daffodils and dwarf orange trees splashed colour to the east of the angled rustic bridge. Beyond them, leafy palms stood guard behind clumps of dwarf bamboo and a banana tree dreamed of companionship. West of the bridge a magnolia had been misled into blossoming.

Just over the bridge and immediately facing the main entrance to the hothouses, a Greyhavens ritual was taking place.

The bride occasionally brushed herself to get rid of the rain she fancied was still on her dress. Her groom stood at her side, clumsy in his unaccustomed highland dress, and even more awkward in his newly married state. The best man showed more confidence, but was more interested in making the acquaintance of the statuesque principal bridesmaid than in carrying out his organizational duties. The principal bridesmaid, fully aware of this, was not uninterested herself. The junior bridesmaid was overawed and excited.

The photographer's assistant had scurried about shooting several minutes of video, but now it was time for the posed photographs. The photographer himself, neat in dark blue slacks and an electric blue sweater, darted forward and back, taking many readings on the meter that hung from a silver chain round his neck. As he worked, he hummed tunelessly.

Albert the gardener, sheltering in his screened-off area behind the group, peered through a crack in the rustic boarding and smiled benignly to himself. It was always the same. Almost every day there were couples, all wanting their photographs taken on the quasi-Chinese bridge. This time it was Antoine. An hour previously it had been Charlie Livingstone. Before that, one of Livingstone's colleagues. It was like a conveyor belt. The photographers went through their standard routine; bride, groom, bride and groom, full party, bride and bridesmaids, groom and groomsmen—all smiles and artificiality.

He was used to the scene—the flow was almost the same every weekend throughout the year, and even sometimes on the other days of the week as well, especially in spring. He snorted gently and looked up. Outside was darkening, and he could see the rain hitting the glass roof above—why someone should want to get married in the depths of December defeated him. There were enough reasons to celebrate the end of the year. Why not spread the occasions round, and get married in the autumn, say? That was devoid of celebration—except for the start of the football season. He grinned again as he watched the photographer. This one was beyond belief. He found him amusing, though his colleague clearly found him nauseating.

'Him!' Kevin had said in tones of deepest contempt as this wedding party had arrived and he had seen who the photographer was. 'I'm off. Let's go get those back beds ready.'

'OK,' Albert had replied, but, feeling he hadn't had his full statutory tea-break, added, 'I'll be with you in a few minutes. On your way round, you could have a look at the carnivores. They're needing some watering, but there's something else wrong. The Venus Flytraps're looking real peaky. Not enough nitrate, I'd say. See what you think.'

'Aye. Maybe. But if you're too long, I'll maybe get away,' Kevin had said. He had glowered through the boarding once more, picked up a fork and strode off, his stiffened back making him taller than he really was. Clearly the mincing photographer offended his sense of the proprieties.

Albert took off his glasses and polished them with a dirty handkerchief. Once more he wondered absently what had happened. In the past he had heard Kevin speak of the wiry photographer with a degree of respect. Kevin was a regular mountaineer, and was a member of a health club which had an artificial climbing pinnacle. According to him, that photographer had a spider-like ability to go up the most unpromising routes. It was one of the few things that he had offered as a topic of conversation during their breaks. But then, a couple of months ago, that had changed. On seeing Antoine lead a happy couple into the Orangerie, Kevin had turned on his heel without a word and disappeared for the rest of the day. Since then he had not been quite as extreme, but always went to the back of the greenhouses while Antoine was around.

Albert peered through the crack again. Antoine's

assistant, he suddenly realized, was a fellow. The pale face and long bottle-blond hair had misled him.

Albert scratching his warty thumb, and shook his head. Was there no limit to the weirdnesses of modern youth, he wondered. Still, that was not his problem. And it was time he was helping Kevin in the back area, and making sure he did what they had been told to do. That was Kevin's trouble. You had to supervise him every minute.

He sighed. Kevin owed his job to his brother-in-law. Anyone else would have bounced him long ago, even though he was strong and could do a good job when he put his mind to it.

Not that he was lazy. Anything but. Kevin worked well, when he worked, and still found time to go to the mountains regularly.

He glanced again through the crack and decided it was safe to move. There'd be no complaints about the gardener appearing in the background, if he could avoid it. Kevin and he had been chewed out by the Silver Fox a couple of weeks earlier after an irate bride's mother had stormed into his office with incriminating photographs. The ties of relationship had not inhibited Webster when he had summoned both of them to his sanctum.

Albert shook his head thoughtfully. Webster, the supervisor, could be quite nasty when he got going. Silver Fox? he thought. More like Silver Rottweiler! Yet there was no doubt that Webster got the work done. And he looked well, an imposing figure of a man with his great mane of pure white hair. Albert knew someone who had been at school with Webster, who insisted that his hair had gone white as a teenager. He himself had argued that Webster was an albino, but that was easily demolished. Webster had piercing bright blue eyes—very striking with his white mane.

Albert peered through the crack once more. That assistant's hair was so obviously artificial, especially when you remembered Webster's. Silver Fox—Silver Rottweiler, Albert stifled a laugh. He'd need to pass on that crack to Kevin. From what he'd occasionally let slip, he'd appreciate it.

But the thought took him back to his immediate duties. There was a lot to be done over in the far corner of the houses, preparing for the change of bedding plants that was needed there. Kevin would be wondering where he had got to. He picked up a fork and headed away. The wedding party paid no attention.

A few yards to the left of the group, Old John had arrived at the pool just as the wedding party had got to the bridge. He was at the end of his usual circuit of the Orangerie. He'd done the main hall, the Tropical House, gone past the carnivorous plants (which he did not like) and through the Cactus House with its marvels. He'd gone into the new bit, and seen the progress that had been made. Then he'd retraced his steps and inspected the little shop, with its glorious cyclamen. He had succumbed to a pale salmon one, with lots of promising buds. It would make a grand present for his daughter (provided that he cared for it and saw that it was not overwatered) and now stood in a plastic bag in front of him, as he sat beside the pool. That was always fun. The size and colours of the carp in the pool fascinated him as he compared them with the memories of his childhood goldfish in its jam-jar.

The stream chuckled its way under the bridge from the upper pool. Carp swirled to the surface and dipped again, coming and going to the upper and lower pools. John smiled gently as he watched the goings-on among the wedding party. The little photographer was a fusspot. He was a joke, a caricature, small with thin mousey hair, foxy-looking, with his tight-fitting slacks and bright blue sweater. John had seen him often. He'd been around, oh, some four or five years now. Old John knew them all, all the normal photographers. But this was one who amused him with his preciousness. He'd come to the city and made quite a splash. Some didn't like his ways, but he had got himself noticed, and carved himself quite a slice of the wedding business. He'd talked about it with his daughter. 'The man's a freak,' John had said. 'How could anyone use something like that?'

Susan had shrugged. 'Maybe,' she'd replied. 'But he looks like a photographer.'

But maybe his business wasn't doing so well. Antoine had done a bit of advertising on the commercial TV channel recently. John yawned. Where had Antoine come from? John couldn't remember.

He looked back to the pool and leaned forward to touch the surface with the tip of his stick. The water boiled as the carp came to see if the intrusion was edible. John drew the stick back and forth, leading the fish from side to side. His favourite black and gold carp wasn't there. Must be up in the upper pool—he'd be able to check that later, he thought. Once this group had been done, and before the next came in. He sighed, and cast a glance up to the glass high above his head. Was there any sign of that rain stopping yet? It'd been dry when he had come down to the Orangerie, but the rain had come on before he'd been able to leave. He glanced at his watch. It was later than he had thought. Maybe the time had gone in the shop. He pulled his coat loosely together. It looked as if it had gone cold outside and he'd need to watch and not get a chill. The doctor had told him to be careful in cold weather—something to do with thickening of the blood, he thought.

Back at the bridge the photographer was fussing with his Rolleiflex. He danced forward to take yet another meter-reading, and then back to the camera. He peered into it once more.

'Up a bit, darling,' he carolled. 'Hold your bouquet up a bit. And the train. Let's have it a bit more spread to the front. As if you've just stopped and turned. Look regal, my dear. Regal! Get that train spread some more.'

He gestured to his assistant, who scurried forward to make the adjustments.

'Now, my dears,' went on Antoine prissily, 'let's have a smile from you all.' He twinkled across the bridge at them.

The bride's eyes narrowed. She had her suspicions about this photographer. The more he cavorted about, the more she wondered about him. Still, he was relatively cheap—inexpensive! she corrected herself—and her friend Thora had some beautiful photos in her album that Antoine had taken.

The flash went off. She bit her lip, hoping that there would not be too many 'red-eyes' among her wedding pictures, as there had been among Sandra's. Poor Sandra! The wedding photos made it seem Sandra had married into a family of vampires. But then she relaxed a little. The flash was pointed up into that white umbrella. But even so, she wondered.

More photos were taken—more efficiently now.

A phone began to bleep.

Antoine dug the portable out from his equipment box.

'Yes? Antoine here. What can I do for you, darling?' he trilled. He smiled up into the magnolia above.

Despite that the bride heard him say, 'My rates are quite flexible, of course. For an important matter, naturally, they are high.'

There was a pause.

'Higher than that, darling,' he continued. Then he bent and twisted sideways, as if to impose some privacy on his conversation.

She could catch no more. 'I wonder what his real name is,' she whispered to her groom.

He, less intelligent than she, failed to take the point of the question, and frowned in puzzlement.

The bride pursed her lips, and their future showed through.

Old John checked his watch again and decided that he'd better just risk the rain if he was to get back to his daughter's house in time for a cup before the football on the TV. He picked up his plastic carrier with the cyclamen and shuffled round the pool and over towards the door. Antoine had paused. The bride was saying something to her new husband. John caught the look on the bride's face as he turned for the door. 'Poor laddie,' he muttered to himself. She looked a right demanding bitch. And the groom so soft! John pulled up his coat collar, pushed his way through the double doors of the hothouse and set off into the rain.

'I bet he's queer,' the bride hissed to her husband of an hour.

Antoine straightened up. For an awful moment she thought he'd heard her. Then she saw he was looking off to her right. He put his phone down.

'Just a minute,' he said. 'There's someone I have to see. Russell, take over. Pose the bridesmaids, please. Shan't be a moment.'

He waggled a mock-warning finger at the group, and went off. The bride watched him disappear behind a clump of tree-ferns and palms.

'Come on,' urged the assistant. 'You heard the boss. Let's have the bridesmaids forward.'

'With or without the ushers?' asked the bride.

'Whatever you want,' replied the assistant.

After a couple of minutes or so he got the group more or less as he wanted them.

They waited.

Antoine did not return.

The bride got impatient. 'Look,' she said to the assistant. 'Obviously your boss has been delayed. And we've got to get to the hotel. You photograph Madeleine and Priscilla.'

'I couldn't do that.' The youngster was horrified by the suggestion.

'Do it,' ordered the bride.

The assistant appealed to the groom. He shrugged. 'Better do as the lady says,' he said weakly.

The assistant shuffled his feet.

'Come on,' the principal bridesmaid said suddenly. 'I'm getting cold.'

They waited a little longer. The bride began to tap her foot and frown. The assistant capitulated. He photographed the bridesmaids. Then, at the instructions of the bride, he took individual photos of the groom, the best man and ushers.

Antoine did not reappear.

'Right,' said the bride, frowning. 'We'd better leave.'

She turned to the hapless assistant. 'I hope your boss has got a good explanation for all this. In any event, tell him to get the proofs to the Brightside Hotel by six.'

She swept off, the wedding party in tow.

Her dress snagged on the bark of the rustic bridge.

The photos were there on time. A mature woman brought the portfolio of photographs for the guests to scrimmage over. The official album would be selected later—after the honeymoon.

Jane Mason went round the edge of the dance-floor and over to the crowd round the photographer's table. There she waited patiently until there was room to see what was on offer. A small lady, she knew better than to enter that sort of scrum.

The photos were not inspiring. She ordered one of herself

and Alan to give to her mother-in-law, and, after only a brief debate within herself, left it at that. The photos of the couple were unattractive. Besides, as Alan had remarked, it was a question why they were there at the wedding at all. They had known the bride's parents well in the distant past, but had not seen them for several years, and certainly had had little to do with their daughter. Still, there was the matter of balancing numbers.

She sighed, and made her way back to where her husband was sitting. He was leaning back in his chair, watching the assembled company. She could tell the signs. He was 'observing'. The habits of a policeman are ingrained, she thought.

'Do you ever go off duty?' she whispered in his ear.

'How much longer must we stay?' he countered as she took her place.

She smiled at him. The light above was casting shadows over his face, making his crooked eyebrow look more than usually devilish. 'A bit yet,' she replied. Poor Alan! He hated these things.

'What're the pictures like?' he asked idly.

'All right.' She smiled.

He decoded the message. The pictures were pretty poor, but she had bought.

'How many?'

'Just one for your mum.'

'And us?'

She shook her head.

The pictures must be pretty awful, if she wasn't buying one for her own collection.

'Not even one for Eric?' he asked, referring to their son who was in the United States.

Jane's face darkened a little, and Mason regretted the question. Jane was missing Eric. This would be the first Christmas that he had not been with them.

'Pricey?' Mason asked, trying to get out of the difficulty.

She nodded.

'How're Ian and Lucy getting on?' she asked suddenly, properly taking up his initiative to change the subject. 'I haven't seen them since we had them to dinner in . . . what? Was it September?'

Mason laughed. 'You're an inveterate matchmaker,' he observed, then continued more seriously, 'I don't know. He's away to London for the week, if that's anything to go by.'

'It is if she's with him. Is she down there as well?'

'No. At least, I don't think so. He has a week to compensate for having duty over Christmas. He said he thought he'd like to see the run-up to a London Christmas.'

'That's where she comes from isn't it?'

'Yes. But there's no significance in that.'

'I wonder.'

She dropped the subject and looked round for vacant seats in the groupings near by. She was preparing to force her husband to be sociable—he could be if he wanted to be—when his beeper went off.

He stood smoothly. She could see the relief in his face. It might be the escape he sought. He grinned at her, and walked out of the room.

He was soon back.

She could tell from his walk. There was business.

'D'you want to stay?' he asked briskly. 'I'm needed.'

She considered briefly.

'No. I've had enough too.'

On the way back in to town Jane Mason remarked, 'It seems they had some problem with the photographs at the Orangerie. The photographer—whatever's his name—got a phone-call and left his assistant to finish taking the bridal group. Can you imagine it?'

Mason shrugged. 'Something must have come up.'

CHAPTER 2

SATURDAY

1

The next morning Mason drove in as usual to work. He always had paperwork to deal with on a Saturday. The summons from the wedding had been to question a smash and grab amateur whose inexperience had betrayed him. He had seen the television reports from England and thought he too could crash a car into an off-licence store and get away with cases of alcohol. It must have seemed a sure thing, for the proceeds would be readily saleable at the festive season. But he had worked alone, and had hoped to use the attack vehicle as his getaway car.

Fair enough maybe if he had used a big car, Mason mused as he drove. But to have used an old Volkswagen Beetle? He shook his head as he sat at a traffic light. The passenger in the car beside him caught his eye and looked oddly at him, but Mason was used to that. As the lights changed he raised a hand in greeting, and went left. It was not his normal route, but he wanted to have a look at the site of one of the morning radio's news stories before he got in to the office. It wouldn't take long.

He hadn't drawn the story to Jane's attention before he had left, but doubtless she'd be phoning in as soon as she saw the write-up there'd doubtless be in the afternoon papers.

As he expected, the road was cordoned off, but he was recognized and allowed through the barrier.

Pulling in behind one of the two fire-engines, he looked at the mess. Beyond the snaking white hoses was a clump of firemen. He caught sight of the new Firemaster—Johnson, he thought the name was. Or was it Pearson? Beside the Firemaster was the angular Deputy Chief Constable, and what looked like Drew-Drew's new assistant. Must be something suspicious to require the presence of the forensic pathologist, he thought. But it was none of his business. Mere curiosity had drawn him to the scene, and he had his own work to do.

Even so, he lingered a few moments more.

Well, that was that. Jane had said the photographer's prices were on the high side, but she had paid. Cash, probably. A cheque could be stopped, but cash? He wondered what the legal position was. There was no chance of their getting their photos now. Would they get their money back? And what about the wedding party, and the rest of the guests?

'Antoine's' was the simple name above the window. Or at least above what had been the window, and he could only deduce the name from what was left of the sign. The building looked thoroughly gutted. Fortunately the fire hadn't spread through the thick granite walls to the row of tenements beside it. He wondered where their occupants had been housed overnight, for clearly they would have been evacuated. But the fire had been confined to the smaller building. That was something.

A mess. A real mess. Pity! But these things happen. Presumably Antoine had been alerted hours ago. He hoped he was insured.

Mason shrugged, started the engine and prepared to move.

The Deputy Chief looked over and raised a peremptory hand, flagging him to stop. Mason wound down his window as he came over to the car.

'And where are you going?' asked the DCC, leaning down to speak.

'In to work.'

'Ah! You've not had my message?'

'What message?'

'You're needed here,' said the other, straightening and opening the car door. 'I asked them to send you out as soon as you came in.'

Mason switched off the engine and got out. 'What's the problem?' he asked.

'Your forensic friend, Drew, is inside. He'll show you. Then have a talk with Bert Johnston.'

Mason pulled his raincoat together, buttoned it, for there was a chill wind, and followed the DCC across to the scene of the fire.

'All yours,' smiled the DCC, and left him at what had been the doorway to the shop.

'Ah, there you are.' A. N. Drew's greeting was warm. 'I thought this one might be put your way.' He waved a black rubber torch at Mason. 'No rest for the wicked.'

Mason looked quizzically at his old friend. 'I never like that kind of phrase on your lips,' he replied wryly. 'What's suspicious?' He knew that a simple fire would not merit the attention of a superintendent.

The corner of Drew's mouth turned down. 'As to cause, you'd better have a word with Johnston about what they've found up here.' He turned and walked to the back of the shop. 'But there's something else. I'm afraid there's someone downstairs.'

Mason nodded, not needing further explanation. A body at the scene of a fire made it a suspicious death. The police would be bound to be involved, even if later it proved to be an accident. There was reason for him to be involved.

Antoine, he supposed. He wondered what had happened that the man had not been able to escape.

As they walked the few paces to the back of the shop, Mason took in the scene. To the left display cabinets had burned and partly collapsed. Beyond them a badly charred steep stair led to an upper floor. Underneath it stood a long machine, presumably for some photographic process. To the right there had been a counter, but it was now largely charcoal. Only at its base did some areas of blistered varnish provide real evidence of what the construction had been. Cabinets against the wall behind it were also a total loss. There had been a carpet. What remained of it was sodden, mushy black.

Drew led the way to a door shape in the rear of the shop. A thin screen-wall divided what had originally been a single shop space. To the right the wall had been partly burned through. Obviously a curtain had been in the doorway but, save for some frizzled remains round the curtain rings, it was gone.

'Nylon?' he asked. Drew paid no attention.

'This was the studio,' observed Drew, going through into an area about twenty feet deep and the full width of the shop. This room was also badly charred, though there was more left of it than the front shop. A couch was pushed against the right-hand side wall. To one side a paunchy red chair still sported some gilt on its wooden moulding. Two tripods lay on the floor.

'How long had it been burning when the Brigade got here?' asked Mason.

'I'm not sure,' Drew replied. 'You'd better ask them.'

'When did you get here?' Mason stood in the middle of the studio and swivelled on one heel to take in the whole picture.

''Bout half an hour ago, I should think.'

The walls had probably been a light cream, the roof

marled—so as to reflect and diffuse light, Mason deduced. There was a large window at the back. He went over to it. It looked out over the steep valley spanned by the Viaduct. Thick cream drapes had been pulled back. The fire had blackened them in streaks. The window was double-glazed, and had a security screen on its outside. He tapped the glass. The window was secure.

'It's fixed. Toughened glass. Rigid. And thick.' Drew's voice came from behind Mason. 'No way out. No way in.'

'And?' asked Mason quietly. He knew what was coming now. There had been recent publicity in the local TV about the problems toughened double-glazing units could cause in case of fire.

Drew pointed to the left-hand corner of the studio space. A section of the floor had been cut out and a spiral stair led downwards.

Drew switched on his torch and led the way. Mason followed.

Below must be the darkroom and workshop or something like that.

'No window?' observed Mason.

'I think this was originally storage space,' Drew said. 'Either that, or it's in the roof of the premises below. They enter from the Glen.'

Mason conjured from memory a picture of the topography of the Viaduct and the Glen it spanned. 'You may be right,' he replied.

Reaching the bottom of the spiral, Drew ran the torch-beam over the walls and contents. Mason stood a couple of steps above him. There were cabinets, steel shelving, some with boxes and bottles of chemicals on them, others with frames and glass. A worktable standing in the middle, but towards the back was clearly where the framing was done. At what was under the front of the shop upstairs was another plasterboard wall with another curtain over its doorway. A neat plastic sign to one side said, 'Darkroom. Keep Out.'

'So?' said Mason, coming off the stairs. 'What caused the fire? It's not gas. That'd have taken the building down. Any view as to cause?' He walked forward, Drew shining the torch on the roof so as not to dazzle him. Mason glanced at the steel shelving as he passed. On a lower shelf were a pair of boots and what looked like a grey and orange set of overalls. As he walked he stumbled against a heap of cable.

'Sorry,' said Drew, now shining the torch on the floor so Mason could see where to put his feet. It wasn't cable that had tripped him, it was a coil of rope.

'Well, there is something upstairs that might be the cause, but I want to do some tests first, and probably call in other specialists,' Drew continued as he ushered Mason along. 'I'm a medic, not versed in the pyrotechnics.'

'No guesses? Nothing to give me a steer?'

'Better ask the experts about that.' Drew repeated his advice. 'But it's up to you and me to form a view on this.' He led the way round the table, then shone the light into the corner beside the darkroom entrance. A light-haired body in a blue sweatshirt and grey trousers lay there.

'Asphyxiated would be my guess,' Drew said quietly. 'We'll see once we get him to the lab, but I'd say he was in the building for some reason, and the fire up above took the oxygen.'

Mason bent and looked at the body. He expected to recognize Antoine, but the face was new to him.

'A thief?' he suggested.

Drew shrugged. 'You do your job. I'll do mine.'

Mason pursed his lips.

'Come on. You've seen the windows,' said Drew testily.

'Was the door forced?'

'I don't think so.'

'Nothing more to go on?'

Drew turned the beam on the ceiling to diffuse the light. 'I think he worked here,' he said quietly. 'There's a sleeping-bag fallen down the back of the couch upstairs.'

Mason went back to the body. 'Who found him?'

'One of the firemen. He's pretty upset. They were doing their usual search of the premises once they had the fire more or less out, and found him just there.'

'Are your people coming?'

'They should be here by now. I radioed back details of what was needed.'

Mason nodded. 'That's right. I thought I saw your new lassie—what's her name? Mandy, is it? She's outside. I'll send her in. OK. You get on with it. I'll go talk to the fire boys.'

'There's upstairs as well,' said Drew quietly.

Having been led to the body, Mason had forgotten the stairs in the front portion of the shop. 'What's up there?'

Drew shrugged again. 'They say there's nothing, and it may not be safe.'

'Who's been up?'

'The fire boys put someone up to check if there was anyone up there. But there was nothing—not at least on a brief check, they say. They took the man down quickly when the frame started creaking.'

'No other body?'

Drew shook his head. 'No. But they'll need to brace it before they do more. The joists are pretty well burned. It's lucky the upper floor didn't come down into the lower. But they don't think there's a body up there. Two rooms. They say one's fitted out in a corner for developing, and the other's another studio. They must be quite big given the size of downstairs.'

'Has Antoine been around?'

'I don't know.'

'Well, despite what the fire boys say, I'd better have a look upstairs,' said Mason. 'Coming?'

Drew sighed resignedly.

'All right. You can go up. I suppose it's safe enough. But don't jump about,' said the officer in the main shop when Mason insisted. 'But you'd better go up separately. Just in case. Them stairs have had a hard day.' He grinned at his own joke.

Thus warned, Mason and Drew were careful in going up the blackened stairs.

Conditions upstairs were as Drew had reported. There were two large rooms.

'Odd,' said Mason, looking round as he got to the top of the stairs. 'Not much damage.' He pointed through the open door.

'Could be the depth of the floor,' suggested Drew, coming up beside him. 'These old buildings are well built. Solid timbering. Takes a lot to fire that.'

'How quick were the firemen on the scene?'

'Pretty fast. Someone reported the blaze from the phone down the road.'

'Anonymously?'

Drew nodded.

'Pity,' Mason remarked. 'So the fire boys were fast, but not fast enough for our friend downstairs.'

' 'Fraid not.

Mason went into the room to the left. Here there was an old-fashioned developing unit beside a sink, and some prints piled on shelves beside it. Apart from the smell of smoke, there was no damage. Mason picked up a print, then another. They were black and white moody studies of a lane, trees and puddles.

Drew followed him. 'I suppose also that if these doors

were shut, that would have helped confine the fire to the middle floor.'

'I suppose so,' remarked Mason, passing the photos to Drew, who looked at them, then put them down.

Mason went and looked out through the window.

'I say! Look at this.' Drew's voice came from the other room. It sounded childishly enthusiastic.

Mason followed him through and Drew demonstrated what he had found. The room was fitted with a series of large scenic prints mounted on roller screens. Clearly it was possible to be photographed there as if one were at Balmoral Castle, in Edinburgh, in a highland glen and various other scenes.

'I've seen that one,' said Mason, gesturing to Drew to pause at a particular background. It was painted, not a photograph, and Mason pointed at some orange overalls and helmets in a corner. 'It looks quite good when it's done right. My nephew was done for his ninth birthday. Phillip on Mars—he's very proud of it.'

'Yes,' said Drew. 'That's a rather nice idea. Better than being taken with the Prime Minister.'

'So where's Antoine?' asked Mason. 'I'd like a word with him.'

'You think he's after the insurance money?' Drew queried.

'Possible. But a bit drastic for someone as refined as he makes himself out to be.'

'No one's seen him today.'

'Curious,' mused Mason.

'Presumably he'll be able to identify the body, when you find him.'

'Presumably.'

The Firemaster and the DCC had come into the building while Mason and Drew were upstairs. Drew went down first, and the DCC brought the Firemaster forward as Mason descended.

'Have you met Firemaster Johnston?' asked the DCC.

'Pleased to meet you, Mr Johnson,' said Mason, shaking the Firemaster's hand.

'Johnston,' replied the other, emphasizing the 't'. 'And I'm sorry we have to meet first professionally.'

'Mm,' replied Mason. 'Our forensic was pretty cagey downstairs. There's the body, of course, but I got the distinct impression that you fire-folk are unhappy as well.'

'Indeed we are.'

'May I ask how? Or why?'

'I'll leave you two to it,' interrupted the DCC. He shook the Firemaster's hand, winked at Mason as he turned away, and left.

'Over here,' resumed the Firemaster. He took Mason behind the counter behind the main window. The counter on this side was blackened, the wood charcoaled and warped where it was not actually ashes. The wall-cabinets were ruined. There seemed to have been a runner carpet on top of the general carpeting.

The Firemaster pointed at a blackened object.

Mason bent to inspect what he was pointing to. It looked like a wine carafe, the sort that Ian Crawford tended to bring when invited to dinner. Beside it the carpeting seemed slimy. Mason rubbed a finger on that patch and then sniffed his finger.

'There's bits of another wine-bottle further over. And a brick,' said the Firemaster.

Mason sat back on his heels.

'It's up to you folk,' said the Firemaster quietly. 'But for my money this was a fire-bombing.'

Mason grunted, and got to his feet.

The Firemaster felt the grunt indicated scepticism, and elaborated. 'First the brick to break the window. Then a couple of bottles full of petrol, the necks stuffed with cotton, or a rag or somesuch.'

'Yes. Yes, I agree,' responded Mason absently, again sniffing his fingers.

Drew came back in with his assistant.

Mason stopped him. 'You know about this?' he asked, pointing to where the carafe lay.

'Yes.'

'OK. Better get on with it,' instructed Mason. 'Let the other Scene of Crime boys in too.'

'Body first?'

Mason nodded and turned back to the Firemaster. 'There's nothing else?'

The Firemaster shook his head.

'Can you leave this place alone now, for a few hours?' Mason asked him. 'You're quite right, I think. And if you were to be spraying more water or shovelling out debris, we might miss something.'

'Take as long as you like,' replied the Firemaster.

2

It was towards lunch-time that the other news came. Drew and his team had almost finished taking photographs, measurements and samples.

In the middle of the morning Mason went in to the office to make sure that his other case-load was properly organized and such as had to be was being coped with in his absence.

He sighed as he got up from his desk. Not that he grudged Crawford his London holiday, but he would have been happier if he could have had him around to deal with some of the detail of organization. He had said as much to the Boss, when he had dropped in to ask how things were going.

'The body's not Antoine?' the Boss had mused.

'No. I've got Paget seeing if he can find him. The odd thing is no one knows where he stays. Don't even know his proper name.'

'Curious,' said the Boss. 'You go on back. See if there's anything come up. I'll see whether I can come up with anything.' He shambled out of the room. Mason smiled at his retreating back. It wasn't often the Big Bear offered to help. But he might more usefully have taken some of the other files off Mason's shoulders.

Mason pulled his raincoat on, and went back to Antoine's burned-out studio. Drew might well fancy some lunch.

When he got out of his car, Lucy Gottman caught him.

'Anything to say, Superintendent?' she asked, clutching her own raincoat round her and waving an arm towards the wreck.

She looked attractively waif-like, Mason thought. As if things were slightly out of control, although she was trying hard, and as if some help would make all the difference to her. Mason smiled. Miss Gottman was not as helpless as she appeared. 'Waif' was an inaccurate term for her build. But here she was. He hadn't seen her for some weeks. Was she back from London? Had she been to London? Although Jane Mason would have loved to know, he did not dare ask.

'I dare say our Press Officer will be able to answer your questions,' he parried.

'You're investigating officer?' she asked, ignoring his reply.

His eyebrow twitched. 'Are you assigned to the story?' he asked.

'Yes.' She looked straight at him. 'Mike Davies is ill, and they thought they could let me loose on this one.'

Mason grunted. He didn't like the sound of that, if she were seeing Crawford off-duty. And he wondered how she had got ahead of others he knew on the *Gazette* who might have had strong seniority claims on the story. Was this down to her uncle?

She decoded his expression, and frowned. 'I know what you're thinking,' she said. 'Uncle Harry's got nothing to do with this assignment.'

'Didn't cross my mind,' he lied.

'In that case you must be worrying about Ian. Rest assured I would never use him as a source.'

Mason kept his face blank.

She turned and nodded towards the door of the studio. An ambulance was pulled up close to it.

'Is there a body in there?' she asked, changing the topic.

Mason was about to parry the question, again by referring her to the Press Officer, when Drew appeared, followed by ambulance men and a wheeled stretcher.

Lucy Gottman stared at Mason. 'Well?'

'One body. Male. Not the owner.' Mason was terse. 'Now you must excuse me.' He went over to Drew.

'We'll see,' Drew answered the unspoken question. 'But I'd expect that it's just as I said. Asphyxiation.'

Mason sighed. 'Well, if you're done here, how about some food?'

Before Drew could reply Mason's car phone started beeping.

It was the Boss. Mason climbed into his car and shut the window. Lucy Gottman might have good hearing.

'Get down to the Orangerie at once. Take Drew if he's free. No. Better take him in any case.'

'Me?' queried Mason. 'Why me? I've just got landed with this Viaduct fire. And there's all those files I've had to drop. I'm still trying to get hold of Antoine,' he prodded, 'but no one's seen him. Nor do I have an address for him.'

'Oh! As to the address, that's easy. You just didn't think of trying the phone book. It gives the studio and home address.' Mason could hear the grin over the line. 'But go to the Orangerie first,' the Boss continued. 'You'll see why when you get there.' The voice had shifted to its 'ironic' setting, and Mason knew better than to argue.

3

Down at the Orangerie, Albert the gardener had gone about his business as normal that morning.

He was grumpy. Kevin had not come in. Of course, that was not unusual. Occasionally of a morning Kevin was the worse for drink and would call in sick. How long Webster would put up with it Albert wondered—he was sure Webster knew. But he himself wasn't going to blow the whistle on Kevin. Kevin had many reasons to hit the bottle, and his brother-in-law knew about them and had done nothing about things in the past. 'Family ties,' muttered Albert.

He sighed and shouldered his tools. In retrospect he could have seen it coming. Kevin had been more than careless late yesterday. Something had been boiling up in that strange mind. But you just lived with it. Kevin had served in Northern Ireland—he knew that. But he never spoke of it, and you never asked.

Take yesterday. Kevin had stomped off when he had seen that photographer. He'd said he was going to the new area at the back. But when Albert had got there, there was no Kevin. He'd just gone off. Without as much as an 'I'm off.' Mind you, if he had said that, Albert would have had something to say about it. So Kevin had just gone. No reason. Nothing. Just no Kevin.

Now he had not come in.

'Still, it's only a Saturday. I suppose it doesn't really matter,' Albert told himself. He tried to make every allowance for his colleague. Saturday was only a morning shift. The general park staff would check things now and then throughout the afternoon, and in due course they would lock up. But Kevin's absence did mean a few things would have to lie over the weekend. With his own bad back, Albert relied on Kevin to do the heavy lifting, and there was some slab-heaving to be done in the new area over at the back of the complex. Albert had hoped to get the short new step path laid through what was to be the herbaceous bed. Pity. All it needed was six granite slabs to be set into the holes he had already dug and sanded. He'd intended to do it with Kevin on the Friday. Kevin had gone off. Now, it would just have to wait again.

Today he could do something less taxing. Maybe he could clean out the poinsettia borders and deadhead the bulbs in the two main chambers, and generally freshen things up.

Yes, that would fill the time nicely till knocking-off. It'd get a job done, and on Monday they could start on the path right away.

That decided, Albert set off for the back beds first, intending to work his way clockwise round the several connected houses.

What felt like some considerable time later and by then well round into the front chamber, Albert sighed and straightened to ease his back. He checked his watch. Only half-eleven! He had had his tea-break, and was making sure that the narcissi were properly staked and tied. He'd probably be able to spin the task out to fill the rest of the morning. Still, last week Webster had told him to check the orchids every Saturday. He'd need to remember to do that as well.

As usual, Old John, out on his constitutional, stopped to pass the time of day.

'There's aye something,' observed Old John. 'Reminds

me of when I had a garden. There was always something needing to be done.'

Albert nodded. Old John rarely required a fuller response.

'I prefer the daffs,' John went on. He pointed with his stick to where the hyacinth and daffodil beds lay. 'That's a right sight.' Then he swung back to the narcissi. 'They're too pale. Who decides what goes in?'

'Webster. Supervisor,' grunted Albert, still tying as he spoke. Then he straightened so as to speak more easily. 'I'd agree with you. But there's no use me saying anything. He's the boss.' He jerked his head towards the rear of the complex. 'Not that he's ever here. He's got a fancy office up at the headquarters.'

'Why's that?' asked John. 'This is where the work is.'

Albert snorted. 'You'd think so.' He bent to his work again. He worked on in silence, but Old John did not move, so Albert continued in a grudging tone, 'I suppose there's some sense in it. He's got more than this place to look after, and if he wasn't somewhere central it'd be more difficult to run things.'

'Oh,' said John. Then, after a pause, 'I was in local government. Before I retired.' He swung his stick, as if to decapitate a pale cream clump of heads. He nodded quietly, and Albert took in the full extent of the unspoken comment. 'Well, I'd better be getting along. Susan'll be looking for me.' Old John turned, and moved away.

'Aye. OK,' Albert responded and bent again to the bulbs. There were still a few narcissus clumps to deal with, and then he'd better go through to the 'sauna' and see if there were any orchids to be deadheaded. Webster might take it into his head to come in today just to check, he thought, and he was death on orchids that were needing deadheading. On Friday afternoon, Albert recalled, there had been some heads, particularly on that salmon pink orchid, that were just getting past their best. And the white spray also had been showing signs of age.

The cul-de-sac 'sauna' that was the Tropical House lived up to its nickname. It was hot and damp, but the plants loved it. And it had been a lot better for them since they had put spring hinges on the doors.

As Albert came down the three steps into the chamber his glasses began to mist. He passed a thumb over the lenses. A glance showed the orchid tree did need attention. Several flower spikes were well withered. He sighed deeply and went back to the cubbyhole for the step-stool.

Carefully he placed the stood on the wet stones of the path. Once, just once, he had been careless, and a leg had slid into a crack just as he had stretched to a high blossom, putting his weight on that corner. He had been lucky then. None of the plants had suffered. He had managed to rewire the bark and packing back into place on the metal frame, and no one had noticed where he had pulled some of it off as he had fallen. He looked, as he always did, at the place. It was quite inconspicuous. But if you got really close you could see the bark and wiring, and even on occasion the metal frame behind. He was always amazed everyone thought the orchids grew on a real tree.

'Better sure than sorry,' he muttered as he unshipped the steps and got up on the stool.

He pulled his old sharp knife from the pocket of his dungarees, stretched up and carefully removed several sprays from the salmon orchid. It had been beautiful that year, and, with luck, his attentions would encourage it to produce at least another couple of sprays before the season ended.

He dropped the cut flowers to the floor, and swivelled to deal with the long sprays of small white flowers of the

'Falling Rain'. It too would benefit from a trim. Maybe he could get at it without moving the stool?

His glasses were again misting up with the humidity. He paused to run a finger over the lens. That helped.

He put his chest against the main side-branch of the tree to steady himself, and reached out.

He pulled the nearer spray towards him, and brought it close for cutting. 'Short back and sides?' he asked it.

Odd! In the background—no, down on the ground at the side wall, under the heating elements—was something blue. Someone must have left a plastic fertilizer bag lying.

He finished attending to the white orchid. He'd need to move the stool for the others.

He got down and carried the stool round the tree and in among the plants in the bed there so that he could get at the other orchids. The flowerbed was shaped into a small mound.

But from there he could see that what was under the heating pipes was not a plastic bag.

CHAPTER 3

MONDAY A.M.

1

Promptly at 9.0 a.m. on the Monday Ian Crawford came into Mason's office.

'You're back, then?' came the greeting, terse as usual.

'I couldn't keep away,' responded Crawford, with a smile. Actually, on his return a yellow Post-It note on his desk had said Mason was waiting for him. As he read it Crawford sighed. Once he had thought the idea excellent, but since Mason had discovered the joys of sticking little notes on his desk, he would have given quite a sum for the chance to tell the inventor of the yellow plague exactly what he thought of him and his invention.

'Good time in London?' Mason's tone was clipped.

'Not bad.' Crawford had learned not to be too forthcoming at the start of a conversation.

'Bankrupt?'

'Somewhat.'

Mason nodded. Crawford seemed subdued, but that was probably the effect of coming in to work. Being on duty and the realization that holiday was over damped many spirits. Further, this new period of duty would extend over Christmas, and might be heavy depending on the incidence of 'flu—and a bad period was forecast. For a moment Mason contemplated inquiring how Lucy Gottman was, but dismissed the thought immediately. What Crawford did off-duty was none of his business, much though Jane

Mason would like to know how (or whether) the romance she had detected was progressing.

Instead Mason got down to business. 'We've got a nasty one on our hands,' he began without further preamble. 'That flashy photographer, Antoine, was garrotted at the Winter Garden on Friday. He was there to take wedding photos.' Mason held up a hand to forestall comment. 'That night—or rather early the next morning—someone lobbed a couple of Molotov cocktails through the window of his shop at the Viaduct. Someone was spending the night there, and was asphyxiated. We haven't got a formal identification for either of them, but that may come today.'

'Garrotted? Molotov cocktails?' Crawford repeated the terms in a sceptical tone.

'There's no doubt about either. Antoine was killed with the chain of his light meter,' explained Mason. 'It was deep into his neck.'

'Strong fellow did it, then.'

Mason nodded.

'And big? I've seen Antoine. He was a wee man, but even so, you'd need to be big to do something like that.'

'Perhaps. But there are ways to do it.'

Crawford looked at him. Mason was gazing abstractedly out of the window. Crawford wondered what memories had slipped out of his Boss's control.

He coughed gently, then asked, 'What do the press know?'

Mason turned with a smile. 'Are you still friendly with what's-her-name? Lucy?'

Crawford knew Mason's memory was anything but defective, but he played the game. 'Lucy Gottman. I see her now and again.'

'That's right. Gottman. You and she were round for dinner after the Monzie business.' He paused. 'Is she still with the *Greyhavens Gazette*?'

'You know she is.'

'Lucky girl, getting in there.' The tone was casual.

Crawford sprang to the defence, then conceded a little. 'She got in on merit. Though I suppose her uncle being Harry Irwin probably helped.'

Mason twitched an eyebrow, but grunted assent. 'Haven't seen Harry around on this one,' he observed, and with a slight smile looked Crawford full in the face.

Crawford jumped to the right conclusion. 'You mean that Lucy's . . . She's been given this one to handle?'

Mason nodded.

Crawford was nonplussed.

Mason broke the silence. 'You'll need to be careful,' he said. 'Go read the paperwork. You'll not have time to see the video—do that later. Come back and we'll go down and you can have a look at both locations. It'll help me too to see them again. The Scene of Crime boys have done their stuff, but it always helps to see the place even after they've been over it. Kind of crystallizes it in the mind. Makes it solid.' The corners of his mouth turned down. 'Then we can go look at the deceased's place.'

Crawford deduced that these killings had somehow affected his boss. He turned for the door.

'Good to have you back,' Mason added as Crawford went out.

2

It was drizzling as they drove to the Winter Garden.

'It's been like this for a week,' Mason said in response to Crawford's question. 'I was hoping you'd bring some decent weather back with you. What we need is some good sharp frosts, not this clammy damp. It's not killing off the bugs. Mark my words, we'll have 'flu running through the town for a few weeks. Snow'd help.'

'It was just like this down south. Even more so, I'd say,' replied Crawford.

'You don't fancy living down there?'

'Working, you mean?' Crawford assumed the answer and carried on, 'House prices are too high. Everyone seems to travel for hours in and out of work. Besides, they're English!'

Mason laughed. The last part of the answer was cogent for some. But his question had serious purpose. He feared Crawford had begun to think of pursuing his career elsewhere—and he personally would regret that. His concern abated with Crawford's comment, but then revived when Crawford continued after a pause.

'Still, it did look interesting. My uncle was a Met man, and took me into New Scotland Yard. Fascinating place, that.'

As he spoke, Crawford parked in the car park at the rear of the Winter Garden. It was almost empty. Mason stretched as he got out. He rotated his right shoulder-blade several times. There seemed to be a roughness, a scrunching more felt than heard. He grimaced slightly, then saw Crawford's eye on him and spoke to divert attention.

'Not too many folk here, thank God.'

Crawford agreed hastily. 'That's a nice one,' he said, pointing to a deep blue Jaguar parked at the end of the car park.

'Nice for some,' replied Mason. He strolled towards a nearby Range-Rover. 'I've always liked these things, provided you get the best quality interior.' He paused, then sighed. 'Well, we'd better get on with it and not envy our betters.'

Crawford grinned, and they walked round to the main entrance.

Inside the hothouses the standard blue and white police tape sealed the tropical section off from the rest of the building. Mason lifted the tape for Crawford, then ducked under it himself. Behind them, a small group slowed on their way through to the Desert House, trying vainly to catch a glimpse of what was going on.

Crawford firmly closed the door to the tropical section behind him, then looked at his superior for instructions. 'Bit hot in here.' The phrase was delivered as a statement, but the question was clear.

'We have to keep it shut,' Mason responded heavily. He stood on the stairs, taking in the section as a whole.

'And damp,' went on Crawford as the humidity struck. The stones of the path glistened and puddles stood in their depressions. An overturned stool lay further into the area.

Mason led the way down the steps to beside the orchids on their tree.

'That's lovely,' said Crawford, pointing to the white orchid that Albert had been working on.

'Mm. They're supposed to be difficult things, orchids,' said Mason. 'But they are fine, aren't they?'

They lingered a moment, then Crawford started to look around with a professional eye.

'Now,' said Mason, pointing. 'The body was over there, behind the tree.' He walked further down the wet path some fifteen feet beyond the tree and then over a plank that had been laid in a depression between two mounds in the flowerbed. Then he waited, close to the exterior wall and patting his hand on the heating pipes.

Crawford followed, picking his way carefully.

'The body was close in under those heating pipes.' Mason pointed to the spot. 'It was therefore concealed from the door and from casual observers. The gardener saw it only because he had come to do some work on the orchids on the tree. Anyone standing on the path, as they should have done, wouldn't have seen the body for that whatever-they-are.' Mason nodded towards the green and red, fleshy spiky plants that stood on the heights of the raised flowerbed.

Crawford went back to the path. What Mason said was true. The plants looked disgusting to his eye. 'Nasty-looking things, those,' he commented.

'Fitting,' said Mason.

'Guzmania. Guz-mania? Who's Guzman?' asked Crawford.

'Eh?' Mason came back out from behind the plants.

Crawford pointed at a small dark sign. '*Guzmania Roseum.*' He pointed at another. '*Guzmania Amaranth.*'

Mason swivelled. Other signs denoted *Guzmania Remembrance*, *Cherry* and *Omer*. He shrugged. 'Whoever he was, I'm sure I'd not like to have my name tagged to those things,' he said, dismissing the matter.

Crawford took the hint. 'So there was a deliberate attempt to conceal the body,' he said, turning back to look at the orchid-covered tree and the bed beneath it.

'I think that's the reasonable conclusion to draw.'

Crawford inspected the area they were standing in. 'There's no sign of a struggle. Where was he killed?'

'I'm not sure about that. With all this wet, and people's feet, it's difficult to say. It could have been out on the stones—' Mason pointed—'or somewhere else, with the body being dumped there.'

'Footprints?'

Mason tapped a foot on the stones they stood on. 'There's nothing really to tell from these flagstones. The gardener who found the body apparently went in among the plants to prune some of the orchids on this side of the tree. He had that stool to get up to the branches—you can see the plugholes from the feet. Doubtless he also trampled the area, particularly after he saw the body. And there's nothing else that might indicate a struggle.'

Crawford nodded. That was what the preliminary report had indicated. 'No deeper footprints?' he asked. 'If the body was carried there through the plants there ought to be deeper footprints.'

Mason shook his head. 'See for yourself.' He gestured at the spiky fronds. There was nothing there to indicate weight.

'And no idea exactly when?' asked Crawford. 'Drew-Drew's post-mortem report is rather non-committal. Not like his usual.'

'Well, you can feel the reason for that. And see where the body was,' replied Mason, suddenly irritable. Drew had dealt with that question in his report. *Given the temperature and the humidity of the Tropical House, aggravated by the location of the body in proximity to the heating pipes, it is very difficult to estimate time of death within half a day. The usual indicators are rendered quite inaccurate.*

Crawford realized his error. 'Yes. I should have thought of that. But we can get some idea, presumably, from the wedding party? Do we know who they were?'

Mason smiled wryly. 'Be grateful for small mercies. As it happens, Jane and I were guests at the wedding involved.'

Crawford looked his surprise.

'Old friends of the parents of the bride,' Mason explained. 'Not that I'd have thought we were in any danger of getting an invitation. It's been ages since we saw anything of them. But you know what parents are when it's a matter of putting on a social do.'

Crawford knew. His own sister having recently married, he needed no clarification.

'We'll be able to interview some of the bridal party later today,' continued Mason. 'I believe the principal actors are away in Greece for another ten days, but I've arranged to see the best man and we may manage others.'

'What about the photos?'

'Yes. Antoine took a good few. After he disappeared, the bride badgered the assistant into finishing the job.'

'She'd have been livid if her photographer upped and left during a photo session just like that!' Crawford smiled at the thought.

'Quite. But there's a further difficulty. You've not seen the studio yet. There's precious little left of it.'

Crawford frowned. 'Ah. Of course.' Then a stray thought crossed his mind. 'I suppose we are sure that it was Antoine here?'

Mason looked his surprise at the question.

'It's just that you said there was no formal identification as yet.'

Mason was about to reply when the sprinkler system went off.

'Blast.'

The two of them headed for the door, and stood just outside it to shake their coats.

Crawford pointed to a cluster of signs to one side of the door. The main one said TROPICAL HOUSE, and underneath in smaller letters another said 'Sprays activated at 11.0 and 3.0.'

Mason grunted. 'Even more reason for Drew not to be able to estimate time of death. Still, what were we saying?'

'No identification as yet.'

'Yes. Well, that's true in formal fact. We don't know any family or anyone close that ought to do the job. But it's clear enough who he is. Even the gardener who found him identified the body. He'd been watching his antics with the wedding party just before he disappeared. Come to that, even I can recognize the fellow. If all else fails there's the advertising tape from his recent TV advertising. That would be sufficient.'

'That's right,' said Crawford. 'Sorry. I remember those adverts. Pretty lousy, I thought.'

Mason shrugged.

'But going back to the sequence of events, didn't the

gardener leave for another part of the greenhouse before Antoine went off?'

'That's right. He'd something to do in the rear houses, and scarpered during one of the breaks in the session.' Mason paused reflectively. 'He's a good witness, that one. He was quite comical describing the fussy way Antoine arranged the gown and so on. Pity that couldn't go down on paper.'

Mason's eyes suddenly focused beyond Crawford, who moved as the Superintendent came forward and pointed at the signs. Below the others another notice said HOUSE CLOSED. 'I wonder when that was put in place,' he said thoughtfully.

'He recognized the body?'

'Who?'

'The gardener.'

'Oh yes. He reported that Antoine was down here. That's why the Boss sent me and not someone else. I was at the studio when the call came through. Now. Time to go.'

They returned to the main hall to go out and round to the car park. As they did so there came a call from behind. 'Hey! Superintendent! Wait!'

They turned.

A tall figure with a white mane of hair came bustling out of the middle passage through to the rear houses.

'Yes, Mr Webster. What can I do for you?' said Mason. He turned to Crawford. 'Sergeant, this is Mr Charles Webster, superintendent of the District's hothouses. You'll have seen his statement in the file.'

Crawford nodded and shook the outstretched hand.

Webster then turned immediately to Mason. He ran one hand through his hair, the other was stuffed in his pocket. 'I was told you were here. Is it all right to allow wedding parties to use the House again? I've had several inquiries.'

Mason hesitated, considering the various factors.

'You've no idea what chaos you caused, closing the House on Saturday,' went on Webster, shaking both hands in the air. 'Several brides were upset. Quite upset.'

Mason smiled bleakly. 'Not as upset as those that turned up for their weddings and found no photographer.'

'Oh? Of course. I hadn't thought of those.' Webster saw Crawford's expression, shook his head slightly and took a grip of himself. He came closer to Mason, speaking fast. 'There's no reason why wedding parties shouldn't use the House. But you'll need to keep your men out of the way. If there's any reason for them still to be here at all.' His face darkened as he frowned. He swept a hand around. 'After all, you've let the ordinary public back in. But I've had the local Councillor making noises about a constituent's wedding tomorrow. I need to be certain before I give an answer.'

Mason stepped back. He could see the point, and the man was agitated, although reference to the Councillor had overtones of contempt. Mason spoke slowly, cooling the situation. 'Yes. I suppose it's all right to let the weddings in. Our people can come down round the side all right, can they? That'd keep them out of sight.'

'Yes. Yes indeed. I'll show you. They could come through the staff door out to the car park, and down through the Desert House.'

'Fine,' said Mason. 'Lead the way.'

'Time for a coffee,' stated Mason, once they had satisfied Webster. He led the way back to the front of the Orangerie, and out and round to the café situated to one side.

'That bloke seemed pretty agitated.'

'Understandable. He's at the sharp end.'

'I bet there were a few worried mothers when they heard the hothouse was closed.'

'Mm.'

'I suppose the photographers would be in a pickle too.'

'Yes.' Mason looked at the tattered clouds outside. 'It's not as if they could easily transfer to an outdoor site—the Rose Garden, say.'

'What did happen about the bookings Antoine must have had?'

'I'm not entirely sure who thought about it,' said Mason. 'But I gather the Boss got someone to tell local ministers and the Registrar's office. They told any couples involved, and I suppose new arrangements were made, fast. It'll have been a bonanza for the other firms, if they had spare people to send out.'

Crawford grinned. 'What it is to be part of a "caring service".'

'Don't be cynical.' Mason's tone was defused by his grin.

Albert frowned as he saw Mason and Crawford depart. He was working in a corner of a section near the upper car park when they walked quickly past on the outside, and disappeared through the public gate in the car park wall.

Kevin hadn't come in that morning either, and there was a lot to get done. Finding the body had upset him, and he had brooded over the weekend. He was upset. If Kevin had been there on the Saturday, he might have been the one to find the body. There wouldn't have been all that police crawling about. He'd been glad just to make his statement as quick as possible, and get away. All those questions about how he found it—it was simple. He'd gone in and there it was. And all that about when he had seen the photographer last. How was he to remember such things?

It had been a bad experience, and Kevin had dropped him in it. He ought to have been there on Saturday.

He resolved that if Kevin did not show up by lunch-time, he'd phone Webster at Council headquarters. This was beyond a joke. The Orangerie needed two men there just to keep it ticking over. And if Webster was serious about the plans for rearranging the large Temperate House he had mentioned the other week, they would have to take on more men, for the initial re-digging and planting, at least. Maybe if he phoned Webster about that, he'd be able to slip in the news about Kevin's absence, without actually complaining.

He pushed his glasses back up his nose, and bent again to his task. Then he straightened again. He hadn't told the police that Kevin had been in the greenhouse on Friday. It had slipped his mind. He'd been asked to describe what he had seen, and had done that as well as he could. Still, it couldn't be important. Otherwise the police would have asked.

3

At the burned-out studio, the shattered windows had been boarded up.

'I'll see if we can get the electricity on again later,' said Mason as he realized a probable difficulty. 'But in the meantime let's have a look at it.' He took a couple of heavy duty torches from the car's glove-box, and they crossed to the studio. Mason nodded to the constable standing in the doorway.

Inside it was difficult to see. Some light came in through the open door. More light was in the rear of the studio, coming from the double-glazing unit. And they had their torches. But it was inconvenient.

There was a curious air of normality. Ashes, glass and burned timbers had been swept together into neat little heaps. The ruined contents of the display cabinets had also been gathered into piles. In the studio portion at the rear the red plush chair stood where it had. The two tripods had been laid over its arms. The couch had been pulled forward, away from the wall.

'They found the sleeping-bag behind that,' observed Mason.

Crawford nodded, and swivelled, getting the picture. 'So the poor sod was sleeping on the couch when the world exploded?'

Mason said nothing.

'And the fire woke him. Presumably he thought he couldn't get through the flames. Though probably if he had tried he would have managed to run through.' Crawford shook his head, turned, and went to the window in the back wall. He tapped it. He turned to scrutinize the room. 'And there's nothing here to break the glass with.'

'It's toughened in any case. And there's the grille outside,' Mason pointed out.

'So he retreated down there,' went on Crawford, going to the spiral stair and looking down. 'Or maybe there was something down there that he thought he could use to break the window.'

'Whatever. We're not likely to know.'

'And that was it?'

'That was it.' Mason switched on his torch and led the way down the spiral. 'As Drew sees it, the blaze up here took all the oxygen.' He stepped off the bottom of the stair. 'I think he's right.'

'Pretty awful,' commented Crawford, following. 'He'd have known what was going on!'

Mason nodded, grim-faced.'

'And we still don't know who he was?'

Mason shook his head. 'I've never heard of Antoine having a male assistant. He preferred female ones, by all accounts. There was a girl in the shop, and another, maturer woman who does the run to each wedding reception, I believe. But that's all.'

'So it might have been a dosser, or something like that?'

'Perhaps. But that's not likely. Mind you, there was nothing to show that he hadn't broken in. But I somehow prefer the hypothesis that he was in here with the consent of the owner.'

'You mentioned an assistant taking photographs after Antoine went walkabout. Could it be him?'

'Could be. Like I said, I never heard of him with a male assistant, but we'll see one of the wedding party later on. That may help.'

'Keys on the body?'

'No. But there was a key on the counter in front.' Mason turned and pointed upwards in the direction of the front part of the shop. 'The firemen found it when they were tidying up. It had fallen through among the counter things when the glass cracked in the fire, but it fits the lock on the door.'

'You're sure it was on the counter and not down in among the things before?'

'Seems reasonable to me,' replied Mason tolerantly. He was pleased to note how his assistant was testing all the information he was being given for alternative explanation.

'So you reckon he was here lawfully.'

'Yes. That's what makes me think that he had something to do with the business.' Mason paused. 'Or with the owner.'

It was Crawford's turn to nod, but only after a sharp glance at Mason.

In the workshop area nothing had changed. Crawford ran his torch over the varied photography accoutrements on the metal shelving. 'Must be money in all this fuss and paraphernalia,' he said drily. 'When my sister got married my mother spent a fortune on photos, and so did Betty.'

'Betty?'

'My sister. Mum got one of those huge awful padded white albums, and Betty got two just to hold photos of all the guests. The real joke is that already no one can remember all the names.'

'She should have written in the names at once. But you're right. Women criticize each other for all the rigmarole, but will they pass it up when they get a chance?'

Crawford let out a sigh.

Mason glanced at him. Was that sigh a symptom, some sort of foreboding? Was his assistant thinking marriage? And if so, might change of status be accompanied of change of job, perhaps to the Metropolitan Force? Might Lucy Gottman want to return to London? He did not ask. 'The body was over here.' He pointed his beam and led the way.

Crawford looked where the body had lain, the outline picked out in chalk.'

'So, while he was dying here, the owner was lying in the Tropical House.'

'So it would seem.' Mason was subdued, Crawford's thinking aloud allowed him to check off his own reactions to the scene.

Upstairs once more Mason pointed to the piles of burned material. 'I've got Forensic going through what they can find of the paperwork. But the fire's done a pretty thorough job. There's almost no film left. And precious little by way of prints either. The set up they used here wasn't fireproof, and it just went up along with everything else.'

'A pretty hot fire, then?'

'That's a good point,' replied Mason. 'I'll check with the fire boys, but that also adds to the indication that it was deliberate.'

'Insurance job?' asked Crawford, then hastily withdrew the suggestion. 'No. Hardly. Not with Antoine dead.'

Mason shrugged. 'Now come on and see the flat.'

4

Outside, Crawford raised a hand in greeting. Mason looked to see who he was waving to, then nodded at the man. It was Willie Sheffield, a senior photographer with the *Greyhavens Gazette.*

'I hope we're not in that,' Mason called.

Sheffield lowered his camera. 'No. No,' he responded, walking over to speak. 'I'm just taking a couple of location shots. In case you folk manage to find out who did it, and there's a trial.' He smiled.

Mason turned, then nodded. 'It looks quite striking, doesn't it?' He raised his hand against the sun and looked at the starkness of the fire-damaged building, streaked with soot.

Sheffield patted his camera. 'I got a real nice one when I arrived. There was a cat sitting on the pavement looking at the shop. I'll maybe put it in for a competition.'

'Come on, Willie,' said Mason. 'You've got enough of those medals by now. Time you gave the youngsters a chance.'

Sheffield snorted. 'Nah! If they're good enough to beat me, fair enough. But until then . . .' He laughed and moved away. Then he turned briefly. 'I'll maybe see you at the match?' he said to Crawford. 'Usual place?'

'Mm. I doubt it,' replied Crawford.

'Boss keeping you too busy?' asked Sheffield archly.

'I refuse to answer the question on the grounds that it may incriminate me,' Crawford laughed, and got into the car.

'What did he mean by that?' Mason asked as they drove away. '"Usual place?"'

Crawford smiled. 'We're old friends. I was at school with his son, and used to play in their garden across the lane. When I go to games I usually get behind the east end goal.

Willie often lurks there for the half when its the opposition goal. Sometimes he works from half way, but often he comes down, especially if it looks as though there'll be a lot of action there. We have a chat now and again.'

Mason nodded sagely. Crawford was being friendly with Sheffield, perhaps innocently, but he was willing to bet also that Sheffield occasionally was passing on information to him. The corners of his mouth twitched as he wondered if Crawford knew that Sheffield was one of Mason's own better sources.

As he started the car Crawford had a question. 'Who reported the fire?'

'Anonymous. From the box down there.' Mason pointed.

'Identifiable?'

Mason shook his head. 'No. Not really. We can try asking the informant to come forward, but I have my doubts if it would work. People just don't want to get involved these days.'

5

They went to Antoine's flat. It consisted of two small rooms with kitchen and bathroom on the upper floor of a building on the main Greyhavens street. A small, neat sign above the bell said 'Antoine'.

Mason pointed at it.

Crawford looked at it and tried to work out what Mason meant by the gesture. He gave up and shrugged. 'So?' he said.

'That's the only name we have for him. Didn't you notice that in the files?'

Crawford thought back quickly, then confessed. 'No. I hadn't noticed that.'

'One of the holes,' remarked Mason.

*

'A tidy man,' Crawford commented as they looked round. The wooden furniture had neat, clean lines. He pulled out a chair from the table, and sat on it, then got up.

'It didn't look too comfortable,' he said. 'And it's not. Bit too straight-backed for me.'

'It's Rennie-Mackintosh,' said Mason quietly. 'Or, presumably that reproduction that they're doing now down in Glasgow.' He waved a hand at the lamps and a wall-hanging. 'So's that.'

'It's got a nice feel, but I'm not sure I'd like to live with it,' said Crawford. 'It's a bit too formal. I'd always be thinking I ought to have a uniform on.'

Mason laughed. 'That's exactly right. I don't feel comfortable with it either. It's a formal sort of suit and shoes thing.'

'A neat man, then. Well organized?'

Mason put his head on one side.

'Doesn't seem quite right for my idea of a photographer.'

Mason paused, then nodded agreement. 'Yes. He does seem to have been well organized.' He pointed to a corner behind another high-backed chair. 'Try over there.'

Crawford went over. Concealed by the chair was a square metal door an inch or so open. He opened it fully. It was a dumpy home office safe. It was empty. 'That had his business material in it. I have the contents down in the office.'

Crawford got on his knees and looked inside. It was bigger than he expected. 'What was in it? Everything?'

'It was odd. There were important business documents all neatly filed. But there's no correspondence with the tax authorities. There's material about local taxes, water charges and the like—all the stuff on the Council Tax and the new one.' He paused for effect. 'But no income tax documents.'

Crawford got to his feet and dusted his knees. 'Is that

usual? These kind of outfit are usually arguing with the tax boys, aren't they?'

'Precisely! When these outfits argue tax they submit what they say is a full set of accounts, but there's no real record of cash transactions. The actual order book is the only thing that's likely to give a reasonable indication of the business profits, but many of them operate two accounting systems. There is some tax correspondence running back seven years, about a business down in Glasgow, but nothing about here.'

'When did he move up?'

'About five years ago.'

'Would current correspondence have been down at the Viaduct?'

Mason made a face. 'I doubt it. He'd have had the sort of records he'd need to run the business there—bookings, orders and so on, but I get the strong impression he ran the official side of things from here.'

'Why?'

'Just the neatness of the paperwork that was in the safe. I can't believe that he'd split that sort of work and keep part of it down at the shop.' He paused. 'Except that there was nothing about the business here.'

'So you think he was on a tax fiddle?'

Mason nodded. 'I think that's implicit in the material that there was in the safe.' He waved a hand to indicate the room they stood in. 'Also, this is a bit more expensive than one might expect.'

'But there's nothing about his current affairs?'

'No.'

'Might someone have been in here before you?'

Mason raised an eyebrow. 'There were no signs of unlawful entry.'

'Just missing documents.'

'No evidence of that either, I'd have to say. Everything

looked as though it hadn't been touched. There were no obvious gaps.'

'It sounds a lot of work, falsifying accounts or running a double set. Who would do it for him? Or would he do it for himself?'

'Difficult to say. Like I say, there's nothing about the Greyhavens business in the portable safe. The only material is on what looks like an old argument. There's no current tax correspondence.'

'He's maybe got a tame accountant somewhere.'

'That's a fair point. If it's true, there may be someone around who could give us a clear idea of how the business was doing, at least in his eyes. That might be interesting. We could compare that with what's in the files that were in here.'

'How would you find out if there was someone working for him?' objected Crawford.

'He might just turn up on our doorstep when he hears he's lost a client.'

'But not if he's helping in a tax fiddle.'

'In that case we ask around,' replied Mason, with a smile.

Crawford shut up. He knew Mason had his personal network of informers—who might produce that sort of information. He was building that sort of network himself. Mason had been in the business much longer than he had and had an excellent network that had proved its usefulness often in the past.

Mason was smiling at him. Crawford had a sinking feeling—he knew that look.

'So what am I missing?'

Mason's smile became a grin. 'The name. The question of the name. The obsolete tax material is for someone called Robert Robinson. There were bank accounts in the names of Andrew Adams, Brian Black, George Grey, Hiram Hector, Stephen Silver and William White. The council-tax payer for this address is George Green, and there is no one on the electoral register from this address.'

'Aliases all.' Crawford was not asking a question.

'Seems likely.'

'So we still don't know who he is.'

'No.'

There was a pause. 'And if his tax affairs had been here, we'd have a name, because the tax and the social security is tied together,' Crawford said slowly.

'Precisely.'

There was another pause, then Crawford spoke.

'Phone book?'

'How do you think we knew where to come? The phone book gives both the business and the home address—different names, of course.'

Crawford moved over and picked a book off the bookshelf against one wall. He riffled through the pages.

'Don't like the look of that,' he said briefly and put it back on the shelf. He ran his fingers along the other books on the shelf, but did not remove others.

'I want you to find out whether the studio was rented or owned by Antoine,' said Mason. 'According to something in his files, he seems to have been in the process of buying it, but I don't know what the exact position was.'

'OK. Any special reason?'

Mason smiled. 'Of course there's a reason. When we get back to the office you can work your way through the business files that were in the home safe thing.'

'Going to give me a hint?' Crawford could see that Mason was willing to talk.

'As I said, he was in an argument with the tax authorities. It goes back to a previous incarnation down in Glasgow, under a different name.' Mason came across to where Crawford stood, and lifted a book from the shelf below that Crawford had inspected. It was a glossy photography book.

He stood looking at its cover. 'I know I said that these kinds of fellows are usually fighting the authorities, but you'll find the fight in this case may have been real. There was a question arising from his previous business that was outstanding. That might tell us exactly who he was.'

Mason fell silent and opened the book. He turned over a few pages and then went back to the cover. 'Mapplethorpe,' he mused. 'Wasn't there a fuss about his work in America?'

'Don't know.'

Mason grunted and put the book back in the bookcase.

'That tax question?' Crawford prompted.

'Ah yes. Well, I know you backed off down at the studio, but it does cross my suspicious mind as well as yours to wonder whether there is an insurance question involved in the blaze.'

'But he was dead by then.'

'True. But think about it. After all, I wouldn't think the business is worth very much on the free market. But as an insurance loss . . . ? It just might be that he had arranged for someone to set fire to it. I don't imagine he knew he wouldn't survive Friday afternoon.'

Crawford's face was a study. 'You can't be serious.'

Mason shook his head. 'No. I suppose I'm not. But there is something about this that worries me. It's not straightforward. It was just a line of thought that seemed worth exploring. He might have had an insurable interest—would have had if he owned it. Again, there might be someone else with an insurance interest in the property.'

'D'you want me to pursue it?'

Mason paused, then: 'Yes,' he said flatly. 'I want to know who owned that building if Antoine didn't, what the insurance arrangements are, who with, and who gets whatever monies fall due now.'

Crawford made a note. 'If we're into hypotheses, there's something else crosses my mind.'

Mason smiled. 'A short trip?'

Crawford ignored the comment. 'I was talking to Lucy, I remember, about this and that, before I went south.'

'And?'

'We were walking back along the Viaduct after the football match mid-week ten days or so ago, and actually passed Antoine's. We were talking about freelancing photograph-wise, for she has quite an interest in photography. It seems the *Gazette* pays quite well for photos.'

'You'd better not be thinking of carrying a 35mm camera to scenes of crime,' Mason warned, half in fun and wholly in earnest.

'Lucy said there was a bit of a war going on just now among the normal photographers. There's been some interest in it at the *Gazette*, though nothing they'd print, of course.'

'Like?'

'Well, it seems that Greyhavens is big enough for the normal three or four firms that operate. But Antoine had broken ranks, charging significantly lower prices for a wedding, say, than the competition.'

Mason sniffed. 'Gang wars in Greyhavens? I just can't see that.'

'I don't think it goes as far as that,' Crawford said cautiously. 'At least, not in the organized sense. But he does seem to have bust up a cosy arrangement among the older firms.'

Mason laughed. 'Should we report them to that European Commission or whatever it's called?' He adopted a supercilious accent and pose. 'If they're engaging in price-fixing, isn't there a gang of civil servants in Brussels detailed to ferret out and stop uncompetitive practices? Is that not what they're for?'

Crawford grinned but said nothing. He had heard his boss wax eloquent on the iniquities of the European Communities before now.

'Doesn't seem too likely to me,' Mason finished in his ordinary tone, shaking his head. 'All the Greyhavens photographers went to school together.'

'Except Antoine.' Crawford was serious.

'Oh, come on,' responded Mason, suddenly testy. 'I went to school with them too. They'd not do something like that.'

Crawford frowned and pressed on. 'But that might just be it. Suppose they have some informal understanding as to rates and quality of service. How much for what price.' He turned and went to the window. 'If you don't mind, I'll do a little asking around about the financial health of some of the competitors. It just might be that someone wanted to get rid of the rogue elephant, if he was threatening a cosy set-up that just might have been running into difficulties with the recession.'

'By way of murder? In Greyhavens? Come on. Pull the other one,' Mason scoffed, then held up a hand when he saw Crawford's expression turning mutinous. 'OK. There is a body—two bodies,' Mason corrected himself. 'But I can't see commercial rivalry being at the bottom of that.'

'Hm.' Crawford's temper cooled as soon as it flared. 'I suppose it is unlikely. But you keep quoting Holmes to me—all that about "exclude all possibilities and what's left, however unlikely, is the truth."'

'Precisely. But remember what you've just said. The unlikely is the truth only when the possible has been excluded.'

'So where do we start?' Crawford was again the subordinate.

'Well, despite what I just said, it might be helpful to get some idea about the standing of the other photography companies. There is a recession on, and, who knows, the murder in the Orangerie and the blaze at the studio just might be two entirely separate incidents, with coincidence busily at work. But we'll start by assuming they are connected and dispose of that assumption first. It shouldn't take long. You do some asking on the lines you indicated.'

Mason paused, and then decided he had better make explicit what else had crossed his mind as he spoke. His tone was suddenly formal.

'If you use Miss Gottman as a source in this, remember that she is the press, and is assigned to cover this story. Don't get trapped into a trade-off of information. Or any other sort of blackmail that you might be open to!'

Crawford opened his mouth to protest. Then shut it.

'In the meantime, we need to inventory everything that's here,' said Mason in a businesslike tone. 'I decided that, since you were coming back in today, it could wait until you saw the place as it was. Now I'll get Paget to send a couple of folk along to do the listing. You stay here until they arrive. Get them to do a systematic search as well for any other cubbyholes, just in case. Then we need to have all the neighbours interviewed to find out what kind of man this Antoine was. We know damn little about him. And once you've told them what we need, come back to the office.'

'Right.'

CHAPTER 4

MONDAY P.M.

1

The phone rang. Mason picked it up.

'Yes.'

'Ye-es.'

'Yes.'

He put the phone down. 'Paget,' he explained. 'He thinks we'd like to see what they've found at Antoine's flat.'

'I'll get my coat,' Crawford responded. 'It looks like the weather's breaking.'

'White Christmas?' Mason speculated.

Two box files sat on the table in the middle of the living-room.

Paget looked modestly pleased. 'There's a small hatch into the eaves,' he explained. 'There were these boxes in there, round the corner.'

He showed Mason and Crawford the hatch, skilfully set into one corner of the living-room to the left of the window and concealed behind the bookcase which had now been moved. He handed Mason a torch. 'The files were just round the corner. Not where you'd see them on a casual look, but easy to the hand.'

Mason took the torch, knelt and stuck his head into the opening. He withdrew, and motioned to Crawford to do the same.

'Have you looked at these?' Mason asked Paget, going over to the table.

'Yes.'

'And?' He lifted off the top file and opened the one underneath. There were photographs in it.

Crawford opened the file that Mason had moved. It also had photographs, but fewer than the other file. Crawford picked up the top five or six and quickly scanned them.

'You've seen these?' he asked angrily.

Paget nodded and shrugged.

'Pity we didn't know about this before,' said Crawford, flourishing the photographs he held. 'He'd not have had any problems with the tax authorities if I had my way with him.' He dropped them on the table.

Mason sighed. 'I've asked around at HQ, particularly the porn squad. That crossed my mind as soon as I heard we had a dead photographer, but no one at HQ admits to hearing anything about that sort of thing.' He paused. 'Besides, it's not illegal to photograph adults. Or apparently to publish the results.' He pointed towards the bookcase, then went over and picked up the book he had looked at in the morning. He threw it contemptuously on the table. 'They call it "Art" nowadays.'

Crawford picked up the other photographs remaining in the file, riffled through them, and then stopped. He held out one photograph to Mason.

'The mortuary photographs of the second body look very like this fellow.'

Mason looked. 'You're right,' he said slowly. 'Yes. I'm sure that's him.'

'So the fellow in the studio was a model,' said Crawford. 'I wonder how he was paid.'

'Or whether he was paid,' replied Mason.

Crawford grimaced. 'We have no identification yet?'

'No. Nor any reports of a missing person.'

2

Sandy Brown was enjoying himself. Although the bus was almost empty and quite light, it was coping with the snow on the road well. The ploughs would be coming through once more in an hour or so, but there was almost no need. It had gone frosty and the light wind blowing from the right was keeping the snow off all but the most sheltered parts of the road. Still, he could tell that shortly the tarmac would have cooled sufficiently for it to lie. Maybe tomorrow would be a different story if the clouds looming to the north dumped their obvious burden overnight.

He looked over to his right as the road started to climb from the valley bottom up towards the Standing Inn. The river showed blue-grey among the trees, catching the clearness of the sky immediately above. It was either going to be very cold or very snowy.

There was a delivery for the Standing Inn, so he pulled the bus in alongside the door to the bar. As he got out of his seat to open the luggage bay, the rangy figure that had been sleeping in the back corner of the bus appeared, rucksack in hand.

Sandy looked at him, then relaxed. That was right. He had taken a Return to the Standing Inn. Must be a climber.

The figure nodded to Sandy, shouldered the rucksack, and went in to the Inn.

Sandy shrugged. It always escaped him how anyone could take pleasure in climatic conditions like the Grampians in winter. Beautiful photos, yes. But actually to go there?

He got the parcel signed for and left. Garage and the end of the run were only a few miles further. He climbed back into the bus and cast a professional eye over the remaining passengers. They were regulars. There'd need to be no more stops before the terminus at Darroch.

It had grown darker even in the few minutes they had stopped. The tarmac was starting to glisten cold in the headlights. He'd be glad when they came down from this exposed stretch of the road high on the side of the valley. Lower down there'd be less chance of awkwardness with the long wheelbase.

3

In the late afternoon Mason and Crawford interviewed Friday's best man. Brian Laing was a teacher. The mother of the bride had told Mason which school he worked in. Mason phoned and arranged to have Laing collected at the end of the school day and brought to police headquarters.

'Run a check on him,' he instructed Crawford after he had made the appointment. 'There's something not right there.'

Some time later Crawford came into Mason's office. 'Can you give me a transplant?' he asked.

'Why? What of?'

'I could do with either your hunch ability, or your memory. Either would do. Brian Laing was investigated seven years ago in connection with an embezzlement at the Drake Cycle Store. His brother was sent down for two and a half years.'

'Ah,' said Mason. 'I thought he sounded familiar. There was something about the way he insisted that we sent an unmarked car for him. I just wondered.' He shrugged, but was pleased that his subconscious has jogged him. 'There was something in his tone. I thought he'd been in touch with us before.'

'Though I suppose a teacher might not like his pupils seeing him being picked up in a police car from school,' observed Crawford.

'No doubt. But there was a curious defiance in his

attitude rather than the sort of "let's keep it discreet" you might have expected. In fact, I wonder now what might be going on there. It's almost as if he was laughing at us.'

'Or maybe he's still nursing a grudge.'

'Perhaps. Maybe this afternoon'll show which.'

'Did you tell him why we wanted to see him?'

'No. I expected he would know. But on reflection I suppose it wasn't necessarily that clear. I just asked him if we could interview him in connection with a police matter. Straightway he raised the question of transport. Said it would have to be unmarked. I don't think I mentioned why we wanted to see him at all, and he didn't ask.'

'It's an odd reaction, then. If he knew about the murder, he'd be expecting us to want to see him. But not to mention it at all? . . . I suppose he does know what's happened?'

'I don't know. Let's wait and see. Certainly the senior bridesmaid knows. That was clear when I spoke to her. Oh, by the way, I've arranged that we'll go and see her this evening.'

'This evening?' Crawford's disappointment was patent.

'This evening. You'll just need to postpone whatever you were planning.'

'Oh well. Yes. OK.'

Mason watched Crawford leave. Was he off to phone Lucy Gottman?

Crawford fetched Brian Laing from Reception. He was behind the tall man as he showed him into Mason's office. Crawford shook his head slightly, and Mason caught the signal. Laing had said nothing on the way up.

'Glad you could come in.' Mason stood, leaned across his desk and held out a hand to Laing. 'Please have a seat.' Laing ignored the hand and Mason smoothly converted the gesture to indicate the seat Laing should occupy.

Laing's eyes flicked about the office before he looked

briefly at Mason. He said nothing. The chair was a trifle small for his size.

Mason resumed his seat behind his desk. Crawford took a seat in the corner.

'We are investigating certain events of the last three days, and would be pleased if you could assist us,' Mason began.

Laing rubbed his hands together, his eyes on the window. 'What events?'

'Are you aware of any events that might have led us to ask you to come in here this afternoon?'

Laing flexed his fingers, then looked directly at Mason. 'No. Your phone-call was a surprise. But then, that's the way you people operate, isn't it?'

'It has to do with the wedding on Friday.'

'The wedding?' Laing relaxed, and then tensed again. 'What about the wedding. There was no trouble then.'

'Have you not seen the *Gazette*? Or heard the radio?'

'No. Can't say I have. Life's too busy for that.'

Mason's broken eyebrow twitched. 'You certainly seemed to be enjoying the festivities at the Brightside Hotel.'

'What d'you know about that?' Laing was suspicious.

'I was there. My wife and I are old friends of the bride's parents. You were jigging about in great style.'

Laing's eyes narrowed. 'You'd not be calling me in to discuss my dancing abilities. What else is there?'

'You remember the photograph session, down at the Winter Garden?'

Laing snorted. 'Too true I do. Right shambles that was. The bloody wee twerp disappeared. Left his assistant to finish the job.'

'Precisely.'

There was a silence in the room. Then Laing half-rose to his feet, but subsided as Mason leaned forward to put his elbows on his desk.

'You mean . . . ?'

'You haven't seen the papers, or heard the radio? Not even any staff-room gossip?'

'No.'

'I find that hard to credit.' Mason's tone was mild as he sat back into his chair and steepled his fingers under his chin. 'Staff-rooms are positive hotbeds of tittle-tattle. Whatever's going on is bound to come up.'

'The main topic just now is whether the pay offer will be satisfactory,' Laing offered.

'Today?'

'I haven't been to the staff-room today. I was in late this morning,' Laing stated. 'If you remember, you phoned at morning break. You caught me before I could get to the staff-room. I had a message to do at lunch-time. So—no gossip.' He pursed his lips, and clearly came to a decision. He sat forward. 'Unless you tell me what's going on, I have other important commitments.'

'Antoine, the photographer, was found dead on Saturday morning in the Tropical House at the Winter Garden. So far as we know the last people to see him would have been yourselves at the photo session. Tell us about that.'

Laing twitched his head, as if to clear it. 'You mean . . . ?' he repeated.

Mason and Crawford waited. Laing collected his thoughts.

'I am sorry,' he began. 'I didn't know. And I can see why you folk would be interested.' He wriggled himself comfortable in the chair, and began.

'So,' summarized Mason when Laing had said his say. 'You didn't think of going to look for the photographer when he had been gone for so long.'

Laing paused. 'I suppose, looking back, I should have.'

'You were the best man, and the best man is supposed

to see that all the arrangements work smoothly,' Mason pointed out.

'I suppose so.' Laing was grudging. 'But just as I was thinking there was something wrong, Candice ordered the assistant to get going with the camera.'

'Candice took charge?'

'She always does.' Laing smiled bleakly. 'She's quite a girl, that.'

'And you just went along with what she ordered?'

Laing nodded.

'That seems strange to me,' responded Mason. 'Surely the wedding photos are extremely important. Surely you should have gone to see what was going on, even if—or particularly if—the bride was getting edgy.'

Laing shrugged.

Mason waited, staring at Laing.

'I suppose so.' Laing's eventual reply was sullen. 'But how was I to know where the man had gone? It's a big place down there.'

Mason conceded the point. It would have been unreasonable for Laing to have pounded his way round the Orangerie looking for the photographer. 'But you could have checked the loos,' he said.

'I suppose so. But the loos are over the other side, beside the tea-room. He went off the other way.' Laing was becoming aggrieved.

'And he had been called away by that phone-call, so I suppose it wasn't likely he'd have gone to the toilet.' Mason was conciliatory.

Laing nodded.

'Are you sure that he went off as a result of the phone-call?' Crawford interjected.

Laing had forgotten his presence, and swung round to eye him. 'That was my impression,' he drawled, and then pointedly turned back to Mason.

'So where was the body found?' he asked. 'You didn't say. Was it in the loos? Is that why you mentioned them?'

'No. It was round in the Tropical House. The Jungle House, I think it's called.'

'The Tropical House?'

'That's right.'

'Where's that?'

'Down the slope to the . . . As the bridal party was standing, it'd have been to your right, down the passage and then through other doors to the left.'

'Ah yes. That's right.' Laing leaned back, relaxing. 'It's the hot and sticky bit. I remember now.' He smiled. 'It's been ages since I actually was round the place.'

'So Antoine finished his phone-call, put down the phone, and went off. Off to your right.'

Laing nodded.

'And you never saw him again?'

'Neither hide nor poncy hair.' Laing seemed comfortable now.

'Did you hear anything from that area—I mean from where Antoine had gone? Any sounds or anything?'

'No.' Laing's reply was normal, then the implication of the question struck home. He put his hands on the arms of the chair and half rose. 'You mean that he . . . that whatever happened . . . happened just over, down the passage, just . . . while we . . . ?' He sank back into the chair.

'Antoine was garrotted, probably just down the passage from where you were.'

Laing passed his hand over his face. 'From what you were saying I thought he'd died—been found dead, or something. Heart. Stroke. You mean he was killed?' He went white.

Mason sat and stared at him. Eventually Laing regained his composure.

'Who's this?' asked Mason, opening a drawer and, to

Crawford's surprise, pushing the mortuary photograph of the unidentified body over to Laing.

Laing's hands shook slightly as he picked it up. He glanced at it, and then became animated. 'That's the photographer's assistant,' he said confidently. 'He's the one that finished the job.'

'Name?'

Laing handed back the photograph and sank back into his chair. 'Don't know,' he said.

'Had you seen him before?'

Laing shook his head, his lips twisting. 'No idea.'

'I see,' Mason said quietly.

'Well,' said Crawford, coming back into Mason's office after seeing Laing on his way. 'There's not much help there. Except he identifies the other body as the assistant on Friday afternoon. I suppose that makes sense. The assistant might well camp out on the premises.' He paused. 'But there's something wrong about Laing. Too edgy at the start. Too relieved when he found out what he wanted to see him about.'

'Agreed,' replied Mason. 'And?'

'And not at all concerned about the other fellow.'

Mason nodded. 'Yes. He was upset about Antoine, but the sight of that photograph seemed to steady him up. File that away in the back of the skull. I have a feeling we'll see more of Mr Brian Laing, but not on this case.'

He sucked his teeth, thought a moment, and made the decision. He opened the desk and took out a file. He opened it, checked something from it, pulled a notepad towards him and wrote as he spoke. 'Get a statement prepared, and you can go and get it signed. Meet me at this address at eight p.m. It's the bridesmaid's. Madeleine Beebe. She's quite a looker.'

Crawford looked at the address, then stuck the note in his pocket. 'I thought there were two bridesmaids.'

'There are. The second is an angel of all of seven or eight years.'

Crawford nodded, and left the room.

4

The senior bridesmaid was waiting for them.

'Come in, gentlemen.' She stood back to let Mason and Crawford past her into the passage that led to the living-room of her flat. She wore form-fitting slacks and a Pringle sweater. 'Put your coats there.' She pointed at a coat-rack screwed to the wall.

Mason and Crawford shook the snow from their coats and hung them up.

As she shut the door, she peered out briefly at the weather. 'It's nice to see snow at Christmastime,' she said. 'Through there.' She pointed down the passage.

A gas imitation-coal fire burned brightly in an antique red-brick fireplace. Two lights shone in the alcoves at either side of the fire. A leather settee faced the fire with individual seats at either side, and a stool was directly in front of the fire. Magazines were piled at the side of the fireplace. Mason noted a copy of the *Greyhavens Gazette* folded on top of a couple of tabloids.

The men waited until she indicated they should sit on the settee.

She sat on the stool in front of the fire, wrapped her arms round her knees and looked at the two.

'Well, gentlemen?' she said.

Crawford found himself wondering how old she was. She had seemed to be in her early twenties when they entered. Now he was not so sure. There was a certain confidence in her pose, and a thickening here and there, that betokened a few more years than he had first thought.

'I expect you know why we are here,' Mason began, pointing at the newspaper. 'So far as we can determine, the wedding party of Friday afternoon was the last that saw Antoine, the photographer, alive.'

She nodded as well as she could with her chin on her knees. The light from the fire gave a halo effect to her hair.

'I thought it was that,' she said thoughtfully. 'How exciting. To have been in at the kill, as it were.'

'The kill?' Crawford was uneasy at her reply.

'You know what I mean. It's like a film, or some such.' She stretched herself. 'I wondered whether we were the last to see him.' She indicated the newspapers. 'There's not much in these, but I thought it must be something like that.'

'It doesn't worry you.' Mason's tone was flat.

'Good heavens, no. Like they say, "If you've gotta go, you gotta go."' She looked from one to the other of the men. 'You find that shocking?' She laughed briefly and got to her feet. 'Life's here to be enjoyed. It ends for everyone.' She crossed to the sideboard, fumbled in a handbag, and took out a packet of cigarettes. She extracted one, crossed back to the stool, and held a cigarette to the flame so that it lit. Then she turned to the two again.

'So what do you want to know?' she asked, suddenly bored.

Mason took her briefly through the usual name, address and employment, then continued. 'We would be grateful if you would simply tell us what you recollect about the photo session in the Winter Garden. All of it.'

She sighed, shrugged her shoulders and looked at Mason. 'That's dull,' she replied. 'Why don't you ask me what you want to know?'

'It's better my way.'

'Why?'

'That way you don't know what I think is important, and might say things that we don't know already.' Mason spread his hands and looked at them. 'We are still feeling our way about. We don't know what's important. Yet.' He looked up at her and smiled. 'You won't object if my assistant takes notes?'

She rose, shook her head, threw her cigarette into the fire, went back to the sideboard and fetched the packet, took out another, lit it, and began.

Crawford took notes.

'And that's it,' she finished. She had added three partly smoked stubs to those already in the gas fire, but had spoken fluently.

'Thank you,' said Mason. 'So to clarify one or two points. First, you thought that the photographer was acting professionally throughout the whole session.'

'I think he did a good job—a damn good job, considering the way Candice was ordering him about.'

'And you heard nothing of the exchange on the phone?'

'Nothing that made sense. He did seem upset about something that the other side said, but maybe he always reacted like that on the phone. Some folk can be right creeps when they're speaking to strangers.'

'What makes you think he was speaking to a stranger?'

'I don't know.' Her tone was thoughtful. 'Maybe I'm wrong about that. But certainly he wasn't speaking to a friend. More a business associate, I'd say.'

Mason nodded encouragement. 'Why d'you say that?'

She frowned as she concentrated on the middle distance. 'I don't know,' she said after a pause. 'It was as if he was arguing and wasn't quite sure how the other side would react. And I'm pretty sure there was something about money involved.'

Crawford straightened up. Mason controlled himself.

'Money?' he prompted.

'Just an impression. Nothing more.'

'It could be important.'

She chewed her bottom lip. 'Maybe in that case I . . . No. I can't be that certain. It was just my impression. Perhaps the others can give you a better idea than I can.'

'We'll see what they say.'

'Have you seen the others yet?' She was concerned. 'You'll not have to question Priscilla—the other bridesmaid?'

'I would think that will not be necessary.'

She nodded relief. 'I was talking to her mum earlier. Please. She's too young. It would be much better if you don't speak to her. She doesn't know anything about all this.'

Mason nodded.

'Were you pleased with the photos?' he asked.

'I didn't see them. And now with the fire, I don't expect I ever will. Pity. But then that's life.'

'But you thought he did a good job?' Mason was puzzled.

She laughed. 'Oh, I see. I misspoke. I meant: as a photographer, he did a good job. I felt comfortable. I suppose he was fussy, but it felt as if he was taking pains to get the best photos possible.'

Mason nodded.

'You were matron of honour, were you?' asked Mason slowly.

The girl looked at him. The light from the fire caught her neck and cheeks cruelly.

'How d'you know that?'

Mason shook his head gently. 'Just a hunch,' he said.

'We're divorced,' she said, turning away to the fire.

Mason rose to his feet. Crawford did likewise.

'Well, thank you for your help. I'll ask my colleague here

to prepare a statement for you to sign, if you don't mind.'

'I could type one out myself,' she replied. 'It'd be no bother, now that I have some idea of what you want to know.'

'That would be useful,' Mason replied. 'But in any event I'll get Sergeant Crawford here to prepare something from his notes too. But thanks for your time and helpfulness.'

'OK.'

'Oh, there is one other thing.' Mason produced the photograph Laing had identified as one of the assistant. 'Is this Antoine's assistant?'

She looked briefly at it, and handed it back. 'Yes. That's him.'

Mason put the photograph back in his pocket.

She led the way to the door where they collected their coats. As she held the door Mason had one further question while he shrugged his way into his raincoat.

'Would you be prepared to give a statement as to where Brian Laing was on Friday night through to Saturday morning—let's say after the reception at the Brightside Inn broke up?' Mason asked quietly.

Crawford darted a glance at him. Mason was looking, not at the girl, but apparently at the smoke curling from the cigarette in the hand holding open the door.

The girl froze a moment, and then took a deep draw at her cigarette before eyeing Mason cautiously.

'You're sharper than you look,' she said.

'That does not answer my question.'

She smiled, bleakly. 'Indirectly, it does.'

Mason nodded. 'None the less, I must repeat it.'

The woman nodded in a jerky response. The policemen left in silence.

'What was that all about?' Crawford asked as they went down the steps from the block of flats.

'I'm not sure,' replied Mason. 'At the reception on Friday she and the best man seemed to be getting on rather better than the occasion demanded. If there is something not right with him, she may give us a lever to open him up.' He stopped, smiled at Crawford, and then gave him an ironic salute. 'Good night. Thanks for your help,' he said, and walked towards his car. 'I hope it's not too late for your other plans,' he threw back over his shoulder as he went.

Crawford pursed his lips as he watched his superior officer drive off. Then he checked his watch.

Mason was comfortable in his old cardigan and wooden clogs. Mindlessly he watched the television for a while, and Jane stitched away at her quilting in her place on the settee. But after a while she saw he was going to talk. She put her work to one side and waited.

'Ian Crawford and I were speaking to both bridesmaid and best man today.'

'Oh yes?'

'They didn't really have much to say that was of any help.'

'Did you think that they would?'

'It was possible.'

Mason fell silent for a minute or so and then continued, 'Did you see those two together at the reception?'

Jane Mason hesitated. 'I saw them doing their duties, dancing and so on.'

'D'you think there could be anything between them?'

'It's possible,' Jane said after a moment. 'I believe that she's separated from her husband. Has been for a few months. Where did you speak with her?'

'She's got a flat in Chronicle Court. She said she's divorced.'

'Not according to Mrs Elliot.'

'Maybe she doesn't know.'

'Perhaps. Or maybe she was putting a face on it.'

Mason nodded, then sucked his teeth. 'There's too much of that going on.'

'What?'

'Marriage break-ups.'

Jane Mason smiled. 'In your line of business, maybe more than anyone else's, I thought you'd be conscious break-ups are the rule and anything else the exception.'

He smiled warmly at her. 'Cadging compliments?'

She smiled back and picked up her needlework. 'Rubbish! You know what I mean. But the fact is that Candice's mother was less than pleased when she chose Madeleine Beebe as her principal bridesmaid. I mean, after all, one doesn't want a probable divorcee as principal bridesmaid. It's not a good omen.'

'Omen? Are we back into pagan days?'

'Pagan days have been back for a couple of decades. But that's not what I mean, and well you know it. It's just not right to have someone whose marriage has gone bust as bridesmaid at a wedding. Even one that's on the skids isn't proper. She might have been hiding that.'

Mason laughed. 'I suppose that's right. But surely it's not right only if the guests know. I mean, I didn't know anything about what you're saying. Not then. Not at the wedding. And I wouldn't have, if this problem hadn't come up.'

She laughed in response. 'Of course, no one expects the police to know what's going on. Not until it's too late. You come along later and sort out the mess. Pity you don't get involved earlier.'

He shifted, slightly uneasy at the implicit attack. 'It's not the function of the police to rule. We only keep the peace. We re-act, not act.'

'I know. I know. I'm just pulling your tail.'

'Getting back to Ms Beebe, is that her married name or what?'

'I think that's her maiden name. But I don't know. I could ask Becky Elliot if you like. But she'd be bound to want to know why I was asking.'

'I don't think it's that necessary. If I want to know I can check the Council employee list. It's not a usual name. Not like Smith. But I'll tell Ian Crawford. I think she made a hit with him.'

Jane Mason made a *moue* at him. 'I don't think she would be the type I'd want to settle down with.'

'It's hardly your or my business,' Mason pointed out reasonably. 'But getting back to the original question: did you get the impression that there was something going on between those two?'

'Ian?' She deliberately misunderstood him.

He made a face at her. 'The best man!'

'If so, it's at an early stage,' Jane replied sagaciously. 'But I know what you mean. They were interested in each other.'

'Both ways? I mean, equally?'

'Now that's different. Let's just say that there seemed to be some mutuality.'

'D'you think anyone else noticed? Was it that obvious?'

'Not sure about that. But if you noticed, it must have been pretty obvious!'

Mason snorted and turned back to the television.

6

Lucy Gottman was in when Ian Crawford phoned.

Shortly afterwards they were sitting in a comfortable hostelry close to her flat.

'So how was London?' she asked.

'Pretty good. But not a place to stay.'

She nodded. 'I found that too.'

'So many people, all intent on their own little worlds. It's a good place to go for a holiday. But I got the impression that there were an awful lot of folk trapped there.'

She tilted her head inquiringly.

'The hotel was near Euston,' he continued earnestly. 'And in the morning there were these floods of folk passing. I followed the stream, upstream, if you know what I mean. And there was a complete torrent coming out of Euston. Like I said, they were flooding out of the place.'

'A good number would be going down the drain into the Underground as well.'

He laughed. 'Quite. You were right. I made that mistake only on the first day. There's no point in going on the Tube before half nine, if you don't have to.'

'So how did you like it? Did you go to the places I said you should try?'

'Some of them.' He was embarrassed. Their tastes did not completely coincide. Some of the things he had gone to see on her recommendation had been boring beyond belief. 'I liked the art galleries. But the shops . . . !' He shrugged.

'Did you see a show?' She moved her glass on the table top.

He smiled ruefully. 'No. By the time I had trekked about during the day, the last thing I wanted was to go to a show.' He paused. If they had been together it might have been different, but he didn't want to say anything like that. At least not yet.

An awkward silence fell.

'So what's doing up here?' he asked.

'You know very well. Superintendent Mason is dealing with a story I have been assigned to. And I'm going to be very good and not ask you anything about it. On or off the record!' She sat very straight, then relaxed. 'But there are other things going on.'

Crawford nodded. 'Yes. The Boss told me you were on the Antoine business.' He inspected his own glass. 'It'd be best if we simply agree it's off-limits.'

She nodded, drank from her glass, and put it down on the table. She did not look at him.

He briefly put a hand over hers. 'Come on,' he said quietly. 'You know how these things work. If it's off limits, it's off limits. But it's not like last time.'

She looked up at him, remembering. She spoke quietly. 'Yes. This is different. Quite different. You were frightening then.'

He drew his brows down. 'I haven't lost that knack,' he said, mock-seriously. Then in turn he too relaxed, sat back and smiled. 'What else is filling your days?'

'This and that.'

Crawford shrugged. 'Any chance you're free on Saturday afternoon? There's a home game.'

She thought for a moment, then shook her head. 'I don't think I can. I'm getting drawn in to some other investigating things. I dare say you know there's an internal inquiry going on at the Council offices about kickbacks for tenders and such things.'

Crawford sat tight. He had heard Alec Shepherd was involved in some sort of investigation, but he did not know much about it. But any reaction by him might be picked up. He confined himself to a shrug. 'There's always stories like that flying around.'

She laughed gently, and patted his hand. 'I'm not asking for any information, but it might be best to steer clear of that topic as well.'

'We were talking about Saturday afternoon.'

'I've got something to write for the midweek edition next week, and I haven't got round to it because of this other thing coming up. I think I should work Saturday afternoon.'

'Oh well. If you change your mind . . . ?' He smiled.

'I'll ring 999.'

'Or 112.'

'112?'

'It's the new number, now we're in Europe.'

'999 doesn't work?'

'It'll work—for a while.'

She laughed. 'You learn something new every day.'

He laughed in response. 'Well, it's useful to know if you're in Europe.'

'Everywhere?'

'Most, I think.' He was uncertain.

'Thanks. Gives me an idea for an article.'

CHAPTER 5

TUESDAY

1

When Crawford got to his desk Mason was sitting on it. He hung his coat on its peg and turned to meet Mason's eye.

'That was hasty,' Mason said, grinning.

Crawford frowned.

'You're going right back out,' explained Mason. 'So, as you're not stopping, you shouldn't take your coat off.'

'That was funnier the way the man used to say it on the radio,' Crawford commented.

'Probably. Probably. And I can't remember his name either,' responded Mason, getting off the desk. 'But it doesn't alter things. I want you to go and talk to Reg Opie.'

'Any special reason?'

'It seems he's Antoine's lawyer.'

'Ah.' Then, puzzled, 'How did you find that out?'

Mason tapped the side of his nose. 'We have our ways.'

It was Crawford's time to grin.

'In fact someone told me.' Mason jerked a thumb in the direction of the ceiling. 'I came up in the lift with the Boss and mentioned we had that little difficulty. So he told me. Just like that.'

'You're sure he's right?'

'Ian, Ian.' Mason shook his head in mock sorrow. 'You're not suggesting our superiors are ill-informed?'

Crawford's grin widened.

'We'll maybe need to get Opie to cooperate later, so watch how you speak to him. But don't get into any real discussion about the circumstances of the fire and so on—nothing about insurance or such-like. That's a later set of questions.'

Crawford nodded. He knew that they would have to investigate (even if only to exclude) the various possibilities they had spoken about when they inspected the wreck of the studio. 'So what am I asking?'

Mason sighed. 'There's several holes we need to fill. Nothing crucial in the investigative sense, but we need to get the data fairly soon.'

Crawford nodded agreement as he jumped ahead of his boss. 'We still need a proper identification.'

Mason nodded. 'And we don't actually know Antoine's real name.' He spoke quietly, slowly and seriously.

Crawford looked up, then remembered. 'Unless one of that batch of names you found in the safe is the real one.'

'Maybe. We know the names on the papers. But we don't have someone to say that the person and one particular name go together. There must be a basic name, a core, a fundamental.'

'Need there be,' objected Crawford. 'In Scotland you can call yourself whatever you like. There's no reason why someone shouldn't have a variety of names for bank accounts and the like?'

'I suppose that's true for bank accounts,' Mason agreed. 'But for tax purposes there must be a single persona with a single name. If you want to have several personæ—' he accentuated the Latin plural—'the only way you can do it is to set up several companies.'

'Any thoughts, then, about the variety of names?'

'Nothing more concrete than we had yesterday. Either he was paranoid, or there was some purpose which might possibly be illegal.'

'Agreed. Do you want me to raise all that with Opie?'

'Heavens, no! Just try to get the real name from him. We can take it from there.'

Crawford nodded.

'There's the other body as well,' continued Mason. 'I had hoped—maybe expected—someone would have come forward to identify the body in the studio, but no one's taken any interest. If Opie can't help with that, see if you can get a list of employees from him. He might know their names, at least.'

Crawford turned to put on his coat. 'I was speaking to Lucy Gottman last night.' He paused while pulling on a sleeve and turned to confront Mason.

Alerted by his tone, Mason looked carefully at him, then voiced his concern. 'Was she after information about Antoine? "Seeking background", or whatever the modern word for "pumping" is?'

'No. Nothing like that.' Crawford appreciated Mason's line of thought and that made him brusque. 'In fact, she said that she expected I'd be involved in something she was assigned to, because I work for you, and she'd steer clear of it. She didn't even name Antoine.'

Mason relaxed. 'So? Why tell me you were speaking to her?'

'It's something else she said. Before I went off on holiday, something Alec Shepherd was saying made me think there was some investigation starting into some of the Council employees.' He looked questioningly at Mason.

Eyes narrowing, Mason nodded for him to go on.

'We were speaking about this and that. I invited her to the game on Saturday. She said she couldn't come.'

'Diplomatic brush-off?' Mason probed.

Crawford shook his head. 'She's been landed with a lot on her plate—Antoine no doubt included—because a special team at the *Gazette* is assigned to some "investigative journalism" on whatever Alec Shepherd's looking into.'

'Was she asking or telling?' Mason was sharp.

Crawford shook his head, angry at Mason's reaction. 'No. Nothing like you're implying,' he said. 'She's not like that. But I thought someone down here should know that the *Gazette* is on to it. If they're asking questions, it might queer our pitch, if we are actually doing any investigating ourselves.'

Mason nodded again, and spread his hands placatingly. 'Yes. I suppose so. I apologize for any implied slur on your lady friend.'

Crawford shrugged and went out. Mason followed. He'd need to tell Alec Shepherd that news, for Crawford was right. Shepherd was deep in an investigation of Council contracts and kickbacks. It would be a disaster if over-eager reporters spoiled all the careful work Shepherd had put in over recent months.

'Out already?' commented the civilian guard on duty at the car park as Crawford walked past.

Crawford smiled. 'No rest for the wicked.'

'Going out of town?'

Crawford shook his head.

'Just as well,' replied the man. 'I was hearing that there's storms coming down the valley. It's been quite fierce. The south road's blocked from beyond Harry's Bridge, and only the north road buses are getting through.'

Crawford nodded, anxious to get away, but unwilling to cut the man off.

'It's going to be bad,' the man continued. 'It's early for the south valley road to be cut. It's usually into late January, even February, before that happens. So, you mark my words, it's going to be a bad winter.'

'Well, we could do with snow,' said Crawford. 'The skiers have had a thin time of it for—what?—three, four years?'

'My wife's brother's with the buses,' the man went on. 'His run was cancelled this morning, she said.'

'Well, my run's not,' said Crawford, rather more curtly than he had intended.

The guard got the point, and, with a jerk of his head, went back to the warmth of his shelter.

2

The offices of Reginald Opie & Co. were in the top right-hand corner of St Martin's Square. Crawford was lucky. There was a vacant parking spot near No. 8, and he pulled in gratefully. He had been chewed out before now for parking unlawfully while on business in the Square. He looked around as he got out of the car. Sure enough, his former antagonist was the warden on duty. Crawford therefore made an elaborate point of going to the parking meter, paying his money and attaching the receipt for two hours' parking to the inside windscreen of his apparently civilian vehicle. He forbore from greeting the attendant. That was taking things too far, perhaps implying he was conceding that the warden had been right in complaining to the police. Crawford had then tried to rely on his warrant card, but though he had won the battle, he had lost the war. Mason had been scathing.

'Enjoy it,' Crawford muttered *sotto voce*, as he left the vehicle. He glanced up at the sky. It was going that dark slate colour that denotes snow. He pulled his collar up against the wind. The forecast for the area wasn't good, though on previous evidence probably Greyhavens itself would escape. But that guard had been quite positive it was going to be bad.

Reginald Opie, medium-sized and in a blue suit, looked as if he belonged in a cut-price electrical showroom. Nothing was said, but as Opie led him along the corridor to his room Crawford felt Opie's attitude was close to that of a manager confronting an obtuse and ill-founded complaint as to quality of goods. Nearly, but not quite, for Crawford was there on official police business, and Opie was a sharp operator. He had an extensive practice among the more shady side of Greyhavens life, and was not the kind to prejudice the future by unnecessary quarrelling.

Opie motioned Crawford to a seat, but remaining standing himself. There was an old-fashioned open coal fire in a magnificent fireplace. He stood before it, back to the fire and rocked back and forward on his heels, waiting for Crawford to speak.

'We understand that you act for—acted for,' Crawford corrected himself, 'the late Antoine, photographer.'

'Yes.' Opie's voice was clipped, and as on previous encounters Crawford found himself wondering whether English was Opie's native tongue.

'We are investigating the events surrounding both his death, and the fire at the studio on the Viaduct,' continued Crawford. 'As his solicitor, you are well placed. Like I said, any assistance you could give us would be gratefully received.'

Opie put his head on one side. 'I think it would be simpler if you were to ask what you want to know. Given the nature of my practice, I find it strange to be asked to talk to the police without specification.' His smile was without warmth.

'Well, let's start at the beginning.' Crawford took a breath, and plunged in. 'We don't actually have an official identification of the body. Is there a relative? Someone that could act for that purpose, at least?'

Opie went over to a row of filing cabinets, pulled open a drawer and removed a thick file. He crossed to his desk and sat down.

'I believe there is a sister,' he said slowly, turning through the pages of the file. 'Yes.' He pulled out a thick document and tapped it with a well-manicured nail. 'There is a sister. I will need to get in touch with her, of course. You are sure that the body is that of my client?'

'As sure as we can be.'

'In that case, perhaps to save the sister distress . . .' Opie paused. 'Perhaps I could identify the body.' He did not look at Crawford.

'Has the sister been in touch? It would be best if it were a relative who did the identification.'

Opie stared at him. 'I believe that the death was an act of violence. A rather unpleasant act of violence.'

Crawford said nothing. He had not been thinking of that facet. He recalled the photographs. The marks of the chain and the distorted features were not the sort of thing a sister should see.

He nodded. 'You're right. If you can do the formal identification for us, I am sure Superintendent Mason would be grateful.'

Opie waited.

'Can I ask when you heard?' asked Crawford.

'Yesterday. I was driving in to work when I heard it on the local radio. Then, of course, here at the office there were the newspapers.'

'Are we talking death or the fire?'

'The fire, of course. As it happened, I was out of town over the weekend and only got back late on Sunday. I heard the late BBC National News, but the news of my client's, uh, difficulties, was, of course, not of national importance.'

Crawford nodded and pressed on. 'There are several other matters where we think you could be of assistance. In relation to the fire at the studio, particularly.'

Opie stood and moved round the desk towards the fireplace where he took up his former position. 'I have to say to you that I am not sure that I can assist further than on a matter of identification.' He shrugged and turned away. 'I probably should not say this, but I believe that it is possible that my client was sailing close to the wind. Obviously, as his legal representative, and that of the estate, I have to protect my client's interests.

'There is a will?'

Opie pointed with his right hand at the desk. 'How do you think I knew there's a sister?'

'You might have known that otherwise,' said Crawford, striving to remain reasonable. 'Still, there's other questions.'

'Yes?'

'Did Antoine own the property?'

'It was leased.'

'From?'

'From the Kingdom Building Society.'

Crawford was surprised. Opie explained smoothly. 'In actual fact the property used to belong to another client of mine, but he secured a loan from the Kingdom on it in connection with another business project he began some years ago. In the current economic circumstances, he got into difficulties and the title was made over to the Kingdom about a year ago.

'Before Antoine got his lease?'

'As you say.'

'And they couldn't get rid of it? They usually try to sell, don't they?'

Opie spread his hands wide. 'True. But it's not a good time to sell, given that it would need a lot done to it to bring it up to standard. It's over a hundred years old, that building, you know.'

'Was it insured?'

Opie smiled. 'Ah,' he said. He paused, and rubbed his hands together while he thought.

'I am afraid not. We had an argument about that just last week. It was part of the conditions of the lease that my client insured, but he had not renewed the insurance. It was due at the end of November.'

'What was the problem?'

Opie shrugged. 'Cost. I got the lowest tender I could, but he still objected.'

Crawford frowned. 'Had he money problems?'

Opie smiled. 'Not that a measly premium would have affected.'

Crawford moved on. 'There was a body in the studio. We don't know who he is.'

Opie nodded again. 'I saw there had been a body found there and thought you might be asking about that. I am afraid I cannot help you there. Antoine employed women.'

'You know the body was male?' Crawford was suddenly suspicious.

'That information was in the *Gazette* report,' replied Opie dismissively.

Crawford cringed inwardly. 'Is there a list of employees? Did your office do the tax returns? The social security payments? Wouldn't you have a list? They might be able to help. Presumably there'd be tax returns for employees—and maybe even the tax returns for the business?'

Opie came back to his desk and, standing, riffled through the file again.

'There were two employees. A Mrs Regan and a Miss Zara Baradi. Regan worked in the shop, took orders and so on. So did the younger girl. She's a qualified photographer and helped with some of the photographing work. The older one worked in the shop, and I believe it was usually she who took proofs to wedding receptions and so on. That is all the employees. I can give you the addresses.'

'That'd be useful,' replied Crawford.

Opie sat down and went back a little way through the file. Then he took a sheet of paper from one of the desk drawers, copied out two names and addresses and handed Crawford the sheet.

'Thanks.' Crawford folded the sheet and put it in his inside pocket. 'And the tax question?' he asked.

'The tax returns and so on are indeed made up in this office, but I do not feel that is something I can make available to you.'

'We could get a warrant. In the circumstances.'

'I suggest you do that.' Opie got to his feet, and looked expectantly at him. When Crawford made no move to leave, he sat down and leaned back, waiting.

'On Friday, it seems, Antoine had a male assistant with him at the Winter Garden.' Crawford crossed his legs, sitting comfortably into the chair. 'In fact, it was the assistant that completed taking the photographs of the wedding party.'

Opie interlaced his fingers, leaning forward on his desk. 'I was unaware of that.'

'So Antoine must have kept you in the dark? About having an assistant, I mean.'

'You cannot draw that inference.' Opie gestured, both hands open. 'It is quite possible that he was being helped on an informal basis by a friend. I believe that there were indeed several persons that used to help him from time to time.'

'Can you give me any names and addresses of those? We might be able to eliminate some.'

'I can not. I know only what my client chose to tell me.'

'So you are saying that Antoine regularly had helpers. But you know nothing about them because they weren't employees.'

Opie shrugged.

Crawford grimaced slightly. There was still something else he had to ask. He leaned forward, swallowed twice, and asked the question.

'Can you give us your client's full name? We seem to have a number of names for him.'

Opie gave a bark of laughter, and slapped both hands down on the desk. 'Now we have it. You don't even know the deceased's name. Wait till I tell my friends. You don't even know the man's name!'

'Can you help us?' Crawford kept a grip on his temper, knowing he was being baited. 'It would save time, and I don't think professional privilege would prevent you disclosing that. Not in the circumstances.'

'Yes.' Opie was immediately decisive. 'I can give you that information.' He pulled a scratch-pad out of a drawer and, as Crawford waited, jotted the information down, refreshing his memory from the file in front of him.

When Opie passed the sheet over, the name was Anthony William James Merrett. There was also a Glasgow address given.

3

'Well, we need to have a complete picture. See to getting a warrant for the Opie material, including the tax,' said Mason wearily. 'I suppose he's right enough. He ought not just to hand over material to us. And in his case, it'd be bad publicity if other clients heard he'd been handing over material willy-nilly.'

'But he did give Antoine's real name.'

Mason pursed his lips. 'Look. Think about it. First, it's a name. Given the rest we know, perhaps it isn't the real name either. Second, Opie's in a difficult position. He doesn't want us to be automatically hostile, so he helps a little. He's playing both ends. It makes life just that little bit easier for him to be helpful to us now and again. In ways that don't affect his clients—and Antoine's dead.'

Crawford saw the point.

'Right, let me have a go at that name first,' Mason said, drawing the phone forward. 'That's not the name used in the tax dispute down in Glasgow.' He rubbed his hands together. 'Progress! Now we need to know whether there was any hidden reason why friend Antoine came up here. Was he run out of town? Was that why he moved, rather than some self-sacrificing impulse to bring us the benefits of his skills. Let me get a feel for that, before we go on to other matters. You see if you can find phone numbers for the older and the younger employees, or for the addresses. Then you can go out and interview. Better take a WPC with you. But come back and see me first, in case I've found anything out.' He waved a dismissing hand at Crawford, and punched in a number. Crawford smiled as he left. He was willing to bet that Mason was not using 'official channels' at this stage of his inquiry.

'Merrett. Merrett. I know the name,' muttered Mason as he waited.

He smiled crookedly at Crawford when he returned. 'I knew the name Merrett rang a bell. Pity it's got nothing to do with Antoine's case. Merrett was an Edinburgh *cause célèbre* in the 1920s or '30s. He was the fellow who shot his mother in Edinburgh. Got a "Not Proven", and later turned up as another murderer. He finally killed himself in some park or other in Germany—Cologne, or Frankfurt.

'Now let's get back to the time with Opie. You say he hadn't taken any steps to get in touch with the sister, although his client had been killed last Friday?'

'He says he only heard about it when it broke in the local papers. At least, he said he'd heard something on the radio, then got the *Gazette* at the office.'

Mason nodded. 'Did you say there's an address for the sister?'

'Yes.'

'We'd better get in touch with her, then. She'll have to do the identification.'

'Opie did not give me her name, or address. He's going to contact her. But he offered to do the identification for us. I'd be inclined to let him. The body's not a pretty sight.'

Mason raised a crooked eyebrow. 'Did he now. That's not like Reggie Opie—being that thoughtful, I mean. Some information's one thing, but going to the morgue . . . !'

'It's Christmastime.'

'I'm not sure that would mean much to Reggie.'

'And it's a client.'

Mason spoke slowly. 'Yes. I suppose it'd be better if he did the identifying rather than a sister.'

Mason thought a moment further, and then nodded again. 'Yes.' He was decisive now. 'Make the arrangements. You and Paget could go along with him. Or if Paget isn't available, see who else you can get for the purpose. It's only a formality.'

'Right.' Crawford was slightly surprised that Mason was not proposing to be present himself. Then another thought struck him. 'You want me to show him the other body as well?'

Mason considered. 'No,' he said at last. 'Let's take things one at a time. I'd prefer to try the employees first for that one. We can use photographs.'

Crawford nodded acceptance of Mason's decision. 'OK. But there's a problem. I got on to Mrs Regan's number. Apparently her husband has taken her off for a holiday to the Lake District for a week. According to her daughter, she was pretty upset by Antoine's death. They live down near the Winter Garden, and can see the top of the hot-house. Seems she couldn't get away from the thought of Antoine lying there overnight. Apparently it's her habit to walk round the hothouses most summer evenings, and the thought of him lying there got to her. So yesterday the daughter and her dad decided that to get her out of town would be useful and they got a cancellation at a hotel they go to regularly in summer. They—Mr and Mrs, that is—left this morning and'll not be back till next Monday.'

'Blast! I take it you got the address?'

'Yes. Beside Bassentwit, or some such name. She spelled it for me. Somewhere down in the Lake District, apparently.'

'Bassenthwaite,' Mason articulated carefully.

'I've got a phone number for the hotel as well if we need it.'

Mason shrugged. 'No point. She'll just have to wait. Back Monday, you said?'

Crawford nodded.

Mason shifted tack. 'And the other? What about her? Any luck there? Has she a phone?'

'Not listed. D'you want me to request a number for the address?'

Mason paused. 'No. No point in stirring up the Telecom

goblins for something like that.' He gestured impatiently. 'Go round and see if there's anyone in.'

'Are you not coming?'

'No. I told you. Take a WPC with you. I want to look up the previous arsons, and go through the file again. Maybe looking at it from the fire end of things will throw something up. We can talk when you come back.'

'And what am I supposed to do?'

'Show the photo. See what she says. But, like I said, take a WPC with you. I told WPC Williams you'd be collecting her about now. And be careful how you edge round to the question of the body.'

Crawford's heart sank at the thought of such a mission. 'You'd not care to show me how?' he asked with a deprecating half-smile.

Mason smiled back. 'Consider it another stage in your education. It's not as though there's anything awful about those photos. He looks as if he's asleep.' Mason patted Crawford on the shoulder, and steered him to the door. 'And you might also inquire about Antoine's relations with his competitors,' he added.

'Why WPC Williams?' asked Crawford.

'Williams is just the right sort of person to have along. Motherly type,' replied Mason shepherding him out into the corridor.

'I know,' said Crawford mock-sorrowfully, mainly, but with an edge in his voice. He had had previous encounters with WPC Williams, who was indeed known among the Force as 'Mother'. 'More like grandmotherly,' he said.

'Very useful,' replied Mason, and went back into his office.

'My gran was an interfering old besom,' Crawford remarked to the closing door.

Mason ignored the comment.

4

Zara Baradi had been watching TV. The set was still on as her mother showed Crawford and Williams into the living-room, but she rose swiftly and switched it off. Mrs Baradi gestured to chairs.

'These police have come to talk to you,' she said to her daughter, and went to a corner chair, adjusting her chaldor as she sat down. Crawford debated asking her to leave, then decided he could live with her presence. There might be advantages in having the mother there.

Zara Baradi sat herself solemnly and faced them. She was in ordinary Western dress. Twenty at most, thought Crawford.

'It has to do with my employer's death?' she prompted them. 'I was expecting someone to call.'

Crawford nodded. 'That. And other things.'

'You've seen the papers?' asked Williams from her seat.

Crawford pursed his lips at her, and she subsided.

Zara Baradi looked at Williams. 'I have seen some of the papers,' she said quietly, turned her attention to Crawford, folded her hands in her lap and waited patiently for the questions.

Crawford took her through the details of her employment, while WPC Williams took notes. Zara Baradi had joined Antoine only in August. She had been looking for a job in the photography line. It was an interest of hers, and she had just finished training at college.

Crawford pointed at a couple of black and white studies framed on one wall. 'Yours?' he asked.

'Yes.'

He went over to them. One, a study of wet slated roofs, was a fine mixture of textures and shapes. 'I like that,' he said.

She smiled shyly, pleased at the praise.

'Was anyone else employed by Antoine?' he asked.

'Mrs Regan.' The girl paused. 'I'm not sure where she stays. Somewhere down near the Garden.'

Crawford turned and nodded encouragingly. 'I'm sure it has come as a great shock to you both. To everyone.'

The girl nodded mutely, and her eyes suddenly filled, but she blinked it away and faced him again, tightening her chin.

'Are you local?' Crawford asked the mother.

'My daughter is,' she replied stiffly. 'Sometimes I think she is more local than the locals. We came from what you would call the "old country", if you were an immigrant.'

'I'm sorry,' responded Crawford. 'I didn't mean anything by that.' Clearly he was close to a nerve.

'Greyhaveners all think that the Customs posts should be put up at Staneport,' remarked WPC Williams placidly, then grinned. Mrs Baradi looked sharply at her for an instant, then relaxed and smiled in response.

'One of the nice things about here is the humour,' she said, and subsided without malice.

Crawford turned back to the girl.

'How did you hear he had died?'

'The radio had the news yesterday. The fire was in the news on Saturday.'

'Have you been to see the shop?'

'Dad drove me round there on Sunday. It was horrible.' She shook her head. 'Do you know what happened? Was it electrical or gas or something?'

'Was Antoine careless about such things?'

She made a face. 'He wasn't too careful. Sometimes he'd have the floods a bit too close to the drapes. They've been singed several times.'

Crawford nodded thoughtfully. 'That's useful to know,' he said. 'It's an idea we've not considered.'

'He was always careless with extension leads as well,'

she went on. 'Sometimes he'd run too many pieces from a single socket with those extension bars, and the plug fuse would go.' She shrugged. She began to pull at a lock of her hair, twisting it between her fingers.

Crawford was tempted to comment. 'You'll go bald if you keep doing that,' he said.

She wound her fingers together again.

'But even if there was some electrical fault, it would need the equipment to be being used for there to be a fire,' Crawford went on. 'There'd have been no one in the shop that night. Would there?'

'That's true. Unless something was already smouldering behind the skirting when the shop was shut.'

'Or someone else went back in? Would Mrs Regan have gone back in to the shop late on Friday?'

'No. I think she was due to go out with the proofs for a wedding. She often did, and when she did she'd usually bring the orders in the next day. But if it was a Friday wedding, she brings them the next week. Saturday is Mrs Regan's day off. Tony dealt with any Saturday weddings himself, usually.' She shrugged. 'You'd need to ask Mrs Regan about that.'

'We will. You weren't in on Saturday?'

'Occasionally, but not usually.'

'Did he ever use you on a Saturday wedding?'

'Sometimes. If there was a clash. But there wasn't this . . .' Her voice tailed off and her hand went to her mouth. She jumped to her feet. 'I just thought. There was a booking for Saturday, and for yesterday and today. There'd have been no one there.'

Crawford calmed her. 'There, there. I understand that was all taken care of.' He turned to WPC Williams for help.

'It's all right, my dear. It's been seen to,' she assured the girl, who sat again.

Crawford took up the questions again. 'Correct me if I'm jumping to false conclusions—Friday is your Sunday, so you weren't in to work that day.'

She nodded mutely.

'It is not required of us,' interjected Mrs Baradi. 'But our family has duties in the mosque, and so it is convenient that Zara does not work on a Friday.'

Crawford nodded, accepting the information. That put an idea into his mind, a way to raise the problem question.

'You said that you and this Mrs Regan were employed by Antoine. But were there any other people doing work—say, occasionally, for Antoine? Or who used to help him? Any regular—' he spread his hands—'helpers? Assistants? That sort of thing.'

The girl frowned. 'Why?'

'There's one or two puzzling things about all this.'

She waited.

He could not read her expression. He pressed on.

'Would you recognize this person?' He passed over the photograph.

She looked briefly at it, then handed it back. 'That's Russell. You're right. He did help Antoine sometimes. Quite a lot recently. But he wasn't employed.'

'You're sure about that?'

She made a *moue*. 'Not that I know about.' She thought further for a moment. 'No. I'm sure not. I heard them rowing the middle of last week. They were down in the darkroom, and I was upstairs. Russell was saying he'd been promised a job, but Tony hadn't done anything about it.'

She took the photo back from Crawford and looked at it again. 'Yes. That's Russell. He's an odd bod.' She gave the photograph back.

'Russell who?' asked Crawford.

She shrugged. 'I don't know. Just Russell.'

'D'you remember anything about him? Anything at all?'

She shook her head slowly. 'I think he might have been a student.'

Crawford was becoming puzzled. 'You don't seem too concerned about your employer's death,' he said gently. He was conscious of Mrs Baradi stiffening behind his shoulder.

The girl unclasped her hands. 'It is the Will of Allah,' she replied.

Crawford wondered whether to hit her with the news the photograph was of a dead man, but decided not to.

'How did your employer get on with other photographer firms in town?' he asked.

'All right, I suppose.' She was indifferent.

'No problems?'

'Not that I know of,' she added more lowly. 'Come to think of it, though, Mrs Regan had some tales of when he was starting. Seems there were some false bookings placed, and false orders phoned in. I was told always to be careful about telephone bookings and orders. Get folk to come in and discuss weddings, and to accept re-orders only if they could give an order number from off a print. Mrs Regan told me that was because of some difficulties there were at the start.'

'I see,' said Crawford. 'That doesn't seem very friendly to me.'

'I believe it does happen when you're starting up in business. There were other stories of that kind at college.' Zara Baradi was quite animated by now, but then her mind caught up with her thought. 'You don't mean you think that some of the others fired the shop, do you? That would be horrible.'

'I don't think it's likely,' responded Crawford calmly. 'But every possibility must be considered when a crime is being investigated.'

She laughed. 'Well, I think you can put that out of your mind. I know the photographers in Greyhavens. They might have done some jokes at the start, but they'd never burn someone out. It's unthinkable.'

'I'm sure you're right,' replied Crawford.

5

'Thanks for rescuing me back there,' said Crawford as they drove away. 'Twice.'

WPC Williams did not pretend to misunderstand. 'Easily done,' she remarked. 'All us real people think of incomers as half real.'

Crawford smiled. He knew exactly what she meant. Yet he had meant his question genuinely. If Zara Baradi were born and raised locally she would share his own attitudes and expectations. That might be important. Yet he had felt that he was not quite getting through to the girl. Maybe the presence of her mother had inhibited her.

WPC Williams seemed to sense his thought. 'Nice girl,' she said, opening up the matter.

'What did you make of all that?' he asked, jerking his head back towards the house they had left.

'Difficult to say,' she replied. 'She's nice, but very young.' She hesitated. 'I mean, a lot younger than her years. Seems to me she didn't quite connect with it all.'

'Was she keeping something back?'

'I didn't think so. Did you think so?'

'Hm. No. I don't.' He paused. Then, 'But she was oddly detached about it all.

'Like I said, she's young.'

'You'd have thought she'd have known what was going on, read all the papers and such-like.'

'Maybe. But has there been all that much in the papers?'

That stopped Crawford. He wasn't sure what had appeared in the papers.

'I take it the matter of the bookings really had been dealt with?'

Crawford nodded. 'Yes. I gather someone high up thought of it, and put out a warning.'

Mrs Williams raised her eyebrows. 'Good for them. Wonders will never cease.'

'D'you think there's any chance the other firms were removing a competitor?' Crawford asked.

Williams laughed. 'Doubt that. His prices were not all that good when you worked out what he was offering. My niece used him the other year. The initial advertised figure looked good, but when you totted up the various extras—he was not too cheap.'

Back at headquarters Crawford reported the gist of his interview with Zara Baradi to Mason.

When he was done Mason simply nodded. He looked tired.

Crawford remembered something. 'Could I see the file again? There's something I want to check in the newspaper account,' he asked.

Mason smiled at the request. He opened the file and pulled out the red plastic folder that held the newspaper cuttings. 'Good for Annie Williams,' he observed quietly as he handed over the folder.

Crawford looked sharply at him, wondering if his lie had been detected.

'Before you went out you said something disparaging about WPC Williams,' went on Mason.

'I didn't!' Crawford defended himself hotly, but Mason raised a quizzical eyebrow, and he collapsed. The charge was just.

'WPC Williams has been here a lot longer than most

of us,' responded Mason. 'She's helped most of us as well.' He smiled briefly. Crawford would have loved to know what lurked behind that flicker of a smile. 'If she said something that helps, take it,' Mason went on. 'But learn to acknowledge that all the best ideas don't necessarily come from under the flat caps. In the meantime, I've been going through the arson cases. We can talk when you come back. I'm going to spin through the fire report again first.'

He waved Crawford out of the room, and opened the file once more.

Crawford glanced at his watch as he left. It was getting late, and he had wanted to see the film on TV that evening.

6

Mason skimmed the forensic report on the studio again but it still brought no inspiration. He turned to the arson summary file, and went through that again. Then he shut it and sat with his hands flat on the file. He had hoped for inspiration to strike, but it had not. A methodical review would have to substitute for inspiration. But it had not really worked. He had put together Antoine and the fire, but he was not fully satisfied with the line of reasoning. Maybe if he went through things again . . . ?

He looked at his watch. Crawford might be a few minutes yet. So he leaned back, and thought, absently rubbing the back of his neck as he did so.

There had been several arson cases in the division in the past few years, but Antoine did not fit their pattern. The others had shared one of three characteristic strands. There had been the loony arsonist who had always used the same *modus operandi*, the candle floating in petrol, with lots more petrol scattered about. He had been identified simply by asking the firemen if they noticed anyone among the watching crowds as some sort of constant spectator. The response had identified one lanky individual in a green anorak as regularly present. When he was spotted at the next fire and challenged, he had crumpled up weeping. He was now a guest of tax-payers' bounty in the local mental hospital.

The second strand was the malicious, vengeful individual. There had been seven such fires in the previous three years. On the face of it, the fire at Antoine's could fit such a pattern, and might still prove to be in series with some of them. But the Antoine blaze had the brick and two fire-bombs. The brick and one fire-bomb made the difference.

The other fires were simple affairs. Twice petrol had been poured through a letter-box and set alight. In one case, the idiot concerned had spilled some petrol on his shoes and trousers while trying to get it through the door, and in consequence had set himself alight. In the other cases a single Molotov cocktail had been thrown. Those cases were still on file. Each involved an attack on a public house, the tentative theory was that they were either symptoms of a protection racket, or some other 'commercial difference of opinion'. Or both, Mason reminded himself. One explanation might not fit those cases.

Antoine was a more calculated occurrence. The brick to break the glass worried Mason. If commercial rivalry lay behind the blaze . . . ? He shook his head. That possibility was not conceivable. He knew none in the photography business would have thought of such a step, let alone have taken it. That possibility was not even a non-runner—it was a none-race!

Unless, he thought, there was a newcomer starting up, determined to make room for himself. Though that seemed an unlikely hypothesis as well. However, he made a note on a pad, lest he forgot.

The remaining possibility was insurance fraud. That explained many arsons everywhere. But that did not seem to fit either. Opie had told Crawford that Antoine had carried no insurance, despite the terms of his lease. Someone at the owner's head office would no doubt be hearing about that, if not actually packing his bags. Still, renewing insurance policies is something that can be overlooked, he mused. Though apparently Antoine had not overlooked it. He had just refused to renew at the best quoted premium.

Unless, he thought suddenly, the fault lay at Opie's door. What if he was lying, and had been instructed to renew, and had just forgotten to do so. There would be no way to prove that one way or the other now.

Suppose Opie had acted deliberately?

Mason chewed that thought around, then gave it up. There seemed no purpose or motive for that. It could be left as a final hare to chase if no other solution came through. Leave Opie. What about others?

Did the owners of the block, the Kingdom Building Society, have some back-up insurance? He paused. That would imply a corporate fraud that was also inconceivable. The studio premises were not all that valuable. Someone with such an intention would have gone for a more expensive property.

'Unless it's a trial run. Unless someone is trying things out, but intent on a big killing somewhere else later,' Mason said to himself. Then shook his head. That was unlikely. Very unlikely.

He snorted gently. There was no fit with previous arsons as to method. There was no fit to fraud. There might be a new loony active in the area. If that was the case, then the police might have to wait until he had struck some more times—the fewer the better!—until they could build a set of clues that would lead to him. Some pattern would emerge.

Alternatively, in the Antoine instance there was some specific cause of malice or revenge to explain the blaze. But if that was the case, would someone burn out the studio after disposing of the photographer? There was, of course, the photographs found in the flat. One of the models? They would have to be traced. But burning a photographer's shop to destroy photographs seemed a very plausible explanation.

Photographs. Photographs. Something niggled there.

He sat back, forcing thought. There was something else trying to coalesce in his mind.

Crawford returned.

Mason put a hand on the files on his desk.

'I spent the afternoon looking through the summary file on arson in the area over the last few years. It doesn't help. It just points up that there was a rather cold deliberation in the attack. The brick and two Molotovs means a very clear and planned intention. I think we have to assume that there is a connection between Antoine's killing and the fire.' Mason leaned back in his chair and rubbed the back of his head. 'That's the only thing that seems to me to make sense.'

'Probably,' Crawford replied.

'Just probably?'

Crawford nodded, and sat forward himself, his elbows on his knees. 'I agree the most likely scenario is that the same person is responsible for both. But until that is established, oughtn't we not to exclude the possibility that we are in fact dealing with two separate occurrences?'

Mason moved his head gingerly—was he developing a stiff neck? 'True, I suppose.' He got to his feet. 'You know I hate that word "scenario",' he added.

He walked to the window. 'If there are two separate

occurrences, then we are left with another question. Why did the fire happen when it did? We now know that there was no fire insurance on the building at all.'

'That leaves only some developer who wants to get into the area. D'you want me to check whether anyone has made a planning application for change of use, or for redevelopment for the site?'

'I suppose we ought not to exclude that possibility,' mused Mason. 'Yes. You do that. Tomorrow.' He came back to his desk. 'But I still think that's not anywhere near a true explanation. It rings no truth.'

'What else is there?'

'Well, I was thinking things over. Forensic is quite clear that there were two fire-bombs, probably preceded by the brick to shatter the glass. That's just them being "professional"—for which read "cagey". But you saw the brick, and the two carafes. The brick shows some very deliberate foresight. Whoever did it was taking no chance on the glass being too thick and the fire-bomb bouncing back.'

'That's not a welcome thought!'

'No. It's not. And the two carafes make it worse. All right, whoever did it may not have known there was anyone in the shop. I could accept that the death was, as it were, an accident—though it isn't for the purpose of a prosecution. It's murder as far as that's concerned. But that apart, there's a degree of planning—shown by the brick and two bombs—that I just do not like. I want to get whoever thought things out that coldly out of circulation for a while.'

'What about rivals?' Crawford waved an arm to encompass Greyhavens. 'Antoine was getting the business.'

Mason came back to his desk. 'Yes. The rivals. What's your reading of that possibility now?'

'I can't see it.' Crawford was blunt. He sat back to explain. 'I can see that there might be some rough stuff to inhibit competition at first, but Antoine had been going for five years and some months. Zara Baradi says she was told there were some attempts to mess him up at first—spurious bookings and orders in the main. But that had passed, though she was instructed to guard against that sort of thing still. It seems he had a niche in the market.' Crawford paused, clearly searching for another strand of thought.

'And?' Mason prompted.

'And it seems his prices weren't all that lower than the competition. Just differently packaged. WPC Williams says he could be more expensive, once you worked out the different costs.'

'Anything else?'

Crawford moved his head from side to side, expressing uncertainty. 'The other thing is that I can't see that any of the rivals would benefit by burning out Antoine after he was dead.'

'Would they have known he was dead? It happened that night. Maybe they had brought someone in, someone professional, to do the firing job. Once that had been set in train there would be no way to stop it. And besides, they wouldn't have known that Antoine was dead.' Mason enjoyed testing lines of argument.

'Possible, I suppose. But I don't buy it. A professional would be completely contrary to local tradition.'

'But not impossible further south.' Mason stood again, then made a chopping movement with his hand. 'No. No. I hope to God it's not that. Let's leave that as least likely.'

'Maybe . . . Maybe . . .' Crawford began twice, and stopped. Mason waited.

'We are assuming that the fire was an attempt to get Antoine out of business. How would it be if someone was just trying to get rid of photographs? Photographs like the ones at the flat.'

'Right,' said Mason, pointing an index finger at his colleague. He had got this far himself, but was pleased that Crawford had done so as well. It gave him confidence. 'That is a real possibility. It's not as radical a thought as that of a professional arsonist. But if someone was wanting to eradicate photographs he, or she, would think burning out the shop would be the way to do it.'

'And it would also keep the link with Antoine's killing as well. If the murder was because of, say, blackmail, then the killer would want to destroy whatever hold Antoine had over him. Probably photographs, Antoine being in that business.' Crawford sat back, satisfied with his thinking.

'But it also leaves open the possibility that the killer and the fire were not connected. Suppose someone heard of Antoine's death . . .' Mason's voice trailed off. 'No. That'd not be the case. The fire happened before the body was discovered.' He stood a moment, then continued, 'I think we're forced to assume that the killer and the arsonist are one and the same. Until we find the contrary, of course.'

'Seems likely to me.' Crawford was beginning to think it might be possible to pack it in for the evening.

'So,' said Mason. 'Tomorrow we have to get someone to go through what's left in the shop and see whether there's a pack of incriminating photos. Some other cache, like that at the flat. Though I'd bet a few hundred pounds that, if Antoine was in the photo blackmail business, he'd not keep them on the premises.'

Crawford nodded.

'And in that case we've got the possible culprits in those box files.' Mason paused. 'And all we know is that one of the models died in the studio fire.'

'We need to identify the others.' Crawford drew the conclusion. 'But we've got nowhere with that so far.'

'The pornography section, or sex crime folk recognize

none of them? Bob was on holiday when I asked. Did he come up with anything?'

Crawford shook his head. 'That's right. It's just as it was. There was only one that was recognized, and apparently he's been down in London for ages, and might even be out of the country. They're checking.'

'Are they now. You didn't tell me that.'

'Sorry,' Crawford apologized. 'I was waiting till that line of inquiry had been exhausted.'

Mason smiled. 'It's not a rebuke. Just a comment. I don't want to be told the detail of everything.' He rotated his shoulders—there was a grinding feeling.

'Wait a minute. I wonder if there's something else,' Crawford said. 'If I recall the inventory from the fire, there was a lot of stuff downstairs that the fire didn't get to classified as "photographic material". It was put into a locker downstairs. Might there be some negatives among it?'

'Negatives!' Mason almost shouted the word.

Crawford looked, puzzled.

'I've been sitting here thinking that if Antoine's killer was also the person who fired the studio, that would be an elegant solution. But I thought that everything was burned.'

'Oh no,' said Crawford. 'Remember the fire didn't get downstairs, and I thought the inventory said there were some photographic materials on the shelves. I'll go and check, if you like.'

He got to his feet and headed for the door. He had just committed the professional mistake of pointing out a possible error to a superior. Mason needed time to recover himself. Going off-duty would have to be postponed.

While he waited Mason let his mind wander. As he did so, a hunch articulated itself. He waited, then grabbed it. A low probability for coincidence of fire and garrotte.

He turned it over, and it remained the same.
He waited for Crawford's return.

Crawford came back to Mason's office in a few minutes.
'So much for that,' he said, flopping down into a chair. 'It's all chemicals. There were also some box files, like the ones Paget found at the flat, but they were empty.'
Inwardly relieved, Mason shrugged. 'It was a good thought. We might have missed something. It's always better to check.' He stood and stretched himself. That shoulder, or the neck, wasn't right. 'Well, I think that's enough for now. We can try again tomorrow.' He smiled. 'You youngsters should know your elders need their sleep.'

CHAPTER 6

WEDNESDAY

1

Opie and Crawford followed Paget and Mandy Bishop into the mortuary.

'Wish I'd put on my coat,' remarked Opie. 'I hate these places.

'Come here often?' asked Crawford innocently.

Opie's mouth tightened. 'Come now, Officer, I am sure you are well aware that much of my practice is in defending those whom society has disadvantaged. I have had a number of clients end their careers here.'

'And some that sent others here?' Crawford spoke clinically, but with a slight edge. He was well aware that not all Opie's clients were as defenceless as Opie implied.

Opie shrugged and waved a dismissive hand. 'It's a jungle out there. Sometimes the survival of the fittest means the perishing of the weak.'

'What about Malcolm Baxter?' asked Crawford quietly. 'He was a client of yours, if I recall correctly.'

'Ah yes. Poor Malcolm.'

'His widow seems to have managed all right.'

Opie stopped and turned to Crawford. 'I hope you are not questioning the Court of Session in its decision that they were man and wife?'

'Oh no. Perish the thought. All I am thinking is that Malcolm Baxter was one whom one would not have expected to have been wandering across a dual carriageway.'

'Yes, indeed. That was most odd,' observed Opie, resuming his pace. 'But the concerted efforts of your Force were unable to come up with any explanation. It was an accident, a complete accident. Your own Forensic folk did the analysis.'

'But he didn't usually drink to excess.'

'Young man, unless you have significant grounds for this line of conversation, I suggest that you abandon it,' Opie said frostily. 'I have never broken the confidence of any of my clients about how they order their affairs. The matter of Malcolm Baxter is closed. It is, if you will forgive the expression in these surroundings, dead and buried. I suggest that it remain so.' He walked on.

Crawford followed, a slight smile on his face.

The grey-green drawer slid out of what Crawford could not help thinking of as the filing cabinet. He motioned Opie closer. The senior attendant lifted back the green cover from the head leaving it folded over the stomach, and stood back. Reginald Opie glanced at the face, turned away towards Crawford, then nodded.

'That's him,' he said.

'You are sure?' asked Crawford, coming to stand beside him.

Opie turned back to the body, and this time looked for a few seconds at it. Then he turned away again and said in an even, colourless voice, 'I formally identify this as the body of my client, Anthony Merrett, otherwise known as Antoine, the photographer. There! Will that do for you?' The last few words had a desperate tone.

Crawford nodded, and signed to the attendant. He lifted his eyebrows at Paget. Paget shook his head.

'All right,' Crawford said to Opie. 'That will do. If you will come back to the office, I have prepared a statement to the effect that you identify the body. It would be useful if you would sign it. Just to keep the paperwork right, you know.'

Opie nodded, pulled a handkerchief from his pocket and pressed it to his lips. He gestured with his other hand at the door, and when Crawford again nodded, left.

'Curious,' was Mason's reaction when Crawford described the identification. 'I wouldn't have thought that Opie would have been fussed about a body.' He started to shrug, then stopped as the shoulder protested. 'Well, you never can tell.'

'I suppose it is a bit gruesome.'

'Strangulations often are.'

'It struck me as a bit odd too,' Crawford said slowly. 'I mean, that Opie was as upset as he was. He started off as bold as brass. He must have had some idea of what he was going to face because that was precisely the reason he gave for identifying for us, and not leaving it to this sister in Glasgow. But then, there's no accounting for tastes. Some might even like seeing that sort of thing.'

Mason grinned. 'You think we should try to balance the budget by selling tickets for the morgue?'

Crawford smiled back. 'You might even be able to get some to pay for the privilege of staying in there all night. Didn't they have people staying all night in Madame Tussaud's Chamber of Horrors?'

'Way, way back, I think.' Mason wrinkled his brow. 'I can't see what anyone would want to do something like that for.'

'Wasn't there some process, centuries ago, that a suspect could be made to touch a body? If the body bled, then that was proof that the suspect was the killer?'

'Yes, I think you're right.' Mason chuckled. 'Imagine getting that method of questioning past the Police Authority nowadays!' Then he became serious. 'Nevertheless, I'm glad you've reported Opie's reaction. You're right. It's a bit odd. Come to think of it, I don't think I've ever had him down in the morgue myself, but I have seen him with bodies. That Cloisters case over on south side. His client had been blown away, but he never turned a hair.'

'That's still on the unsolved list, isn't it?'

Mason smiled grimly. 'Aye. Unsolved list!'

Crawford detected an implication and raised his brows questioningly.

Mason's mouth turned sharply down at the edges. 'Oh, I know who did it. So does Alec Shepherd. But there's just not enough proof. Crown Office wouldn't proceed.'

Crawford was surprised. 'What was wrong?'

'Come on,' said Mason sarcastically. 'You know Crown Office wants to see a reasonable prospect of a conviction before they'll go ahead with a prosecution.'

'What was wrong?' Crawford repeated. 'That was before my time.'

Mason raised a clenched fist. 'One,' he said raising the index finger, 'a crucial witness disappeared, and has never been seen since. Two—' another finger was extended, and his voice harshened—'some evidence vanished.'

'Evidence vanished? From . . . from . . . ?' Crawford was appalled.

'Vanished.' Crawford's tone became weary. 'It does happen, you know. Not all the bent officers are south of the Border.'

'You suspect someone in here?' Crawford gestured to the building around.

'It's a reasonable inference,' replied Mason. 'The evidence was in a locked cabinet down on the Third Floor one day. When we went to get it a couple of days later for the review, it was gone.'

'It? You didn't say what it was.'

'The shotgun.'

'What happened to it?'

'Like I said, it vanished. It could be anywhere. Could be in a cupboard somewhere. Stashed away against a future need.'

Crawford understood and nodded.

Mason straightened. 'But I think it's more likely that it was quietly dropped over the side, somewhere far out, probably off an oil support boat.'

Crawford nodded again, his face solemn. 'Who d'you think took it?'

'Someone. Someone who either wanted to, or whose arm was twistable.'

'Not a policeman?' Crawford was slightly sick at the idea. He thought highly of his colleagues.

'Perhaps,' replied Mason.

'But it could have been anyone? Anyone with access, I mean. Not necessarily colleagues.'

Mason sighed. 'I suppose so. We tracked everyone we could think of, including the cleaners. But . . .' He started to shrug again, and halted the movement abruptly.

The phone rang. Mason picked it up.

'Yes. All right,' he said, after listening a short time. 'It may trigger something to let that information out, but only on an unconfirmed basis. Right?'

He put the phone down.

'Press Office,' he explained. 'Someone at the *Gazette* has asked them to confirm that the body in the studio was Antoine's assistant.' He raised an eyebrow at Crawford.

Crawford shook his head. 'Not me,' he said firmly. 'She's not said peep about the case. And nor have I.'

Mason accepted the denial. 'Tell you what bothers me,' he went on reflectively. 'We really know so very little about Antoine.' He clapped a fist into his other hand. 'We know he took pictures above and beyond the call of business. We also know that he had a number of bank accounts in different names in different branches throughout the city. That's being looked into. It seems that there was a fair amount of money slushing around there. And cash withdrawals, and deposits. But it seems too methodical to me. The obvious question is blackmail, but there's been no whiff of that sort of thing in the gossip.'

He paused and looked at Crawford for reaction, but got no help.

'But there's a big hole at the heart of it all. We don't know what Antoine was like. What did he do when he was off-duty? What were his hobbies? What kind of a man was he? What were his interests? His extra-curricular activities? His friends? Did he have any? We just don't know. He's a blank.'

He went to his desk and opened the file. 'Why does the inventory of the flat include three leotards and some worn trainers?'

Crawford pointed a finger. 'There were boots downstairs at the studio.'

Mason glanced at him, thought a moment, then nodded. 'Yes. On those shelves.'

'And rope.'

'Yes?' Mason was cautious.

'Maybe we should talk to the Hillwalkers, or the Mountaineering Club.'

Mason's mouth turned down. 'Seems farfetched to me. He wasn't that sort.'

Crawford shrugged. 'Suit yourself. But as you said, we're stuck for any information about him other than his work. There must be something else.'

'Suppose so,' said Mason reluctantly. 'Can you handle that?'

'OK.'

'And either you or someone—WPC Williams perhaps—could go back and talk to the Baradi girl and see whether she can shed any light on her employer's extra-curricular activities.

'OK.'

Crawford phoned and made the appointments.

He was in the middle of briefing WPC Williams about her task for the next morning when Mason phoned.

'You'd better come up,' Mason said. 'Albert Strachan has come in with something to add to his statement.'

2

Albert twisted his gnarled hands as he spoke.

'So you see, sir,' he concluded, 'it was only later that I thought over what I had told you and thought it wasn't maybe enough.' He straightened and looked keenly first at Crawford and then at Mason. 'But you never asked me who else was there that afternoon. You only asked me about the photographing party.'

Mason nodded.

'So you've not seen your friend since Friday.'

'No, sir.' The tone was quiet.

'And you think that's important.'

Albert paused. 'I'm not sure,' he hazarded at last. 'But when I watch Inspector Morse and things like that on the TV, it's always that the police have to have all the information they can get.' He paused. 'I didn't want to come in about it. But my Mary said I should. I mean, Kevin is often not there for a day or two. He'd some awful experiences in the past, and sometimes he helps the memories away by the drink.'

'But he's been away longer than usual this time?'

Albert shrugged. He was beginning to think he shouldn't have come. It felt as if he was betraying Kevin. 'No. He's been gone longer than this in the past. But Mary said I should come in. Because of what's happened.'

Mason stood. 'Well, thank you for coming. And thank your wife also for prompting you. It does help if we know as much as we possibly can about these things. And it's my fault for not managing to ask you a question last time that would have brought out the fact of your colleague's presence.' He held out his hand. 'You have been most helpful. My colleague will prepare a short statement for you to sign before you leave. And I expect he'll be able to rustle up some tea or coffee as well.' He gestured to Crawford.

Albert got to his feet. He nodded, grateful that it was all over.

At the door, he turned. 'There's Old John as well,' he said. 'He was there.'

'See what happens when you're not here to keep me right,' Mason said wryly to Crawford when he brought back the statement. 'Learn, laddie. Learn. It's better to learn from the mistakes of others rather than from your own.' He took the sheet of paper and ran an eye down it. 'Anything of interest?'

Crawford waited.

'Did he say anything more about why his colleague goes on the bottle?'

Crawford shook his head.

'Well, we'd better try to find him. And this other one. The old man. He's got a stick, the gardener said. I expect he's most easily found down at the Orangerie. We can get Paget to send someone down to catch him tomorrow morning. And as for the other, the employment record will give us an address. Check that out as well, please.'

Crawford nodded. He had anticipated both requests.

'Did you ask if there was anyone else around?'

Crawford grinned. Mason had asked exactly that

question before he had finally let Albert go, but he had himself confirmed the answer.

'He says there wasn't anyone else about that he saw. It was rather a bad day. "Quite inclement" was his exact phrase.'

Mason smiled in response. 'You know,' he said, 'it's remarkable the command of language that some of these older folk have got. I blame these modern schools. They don't encourage the kids to read decent books any more. "Quite inclement" indeed! It was cold, and damn squally. I almost caught my death of cold standing around waiting to be photographed at the church.'

He paused, then tapped the file. 'Find this Kevin,' he instructed.

CHAPTER 7

THURSDAY

1

'You do know who I'm asking about?' Crawford was impatient.

'Look, Constable,' said the man pursing his lips, 'I know the members of the Mountaineering Club. They're all friends of mine. If I say we haven't got the man you're asking about, then we haven't got the man you're asking about.'

'But he did have climbing equipment in his basement,' persisted Crawford, who had checked the inventory before setting out.

The man sighed. 'It's a free country. Anyone can go to the hills. They don't have to pass a test, or be a member of a club. They don't even have to tell anyone what they're doing, worse luck. That's why half the Mountaineering Club are also members of Mountain Rescue.' Clearly he was exasperated. 'That's why we have to go out and rescue the stupid sods.'

'I know the good work Mountain Rescue does,' Crawford acknowledged. 'We're very grateful to them. Regularly. But . . .' He stopped, uncertain how to proceed diplomatically.

'But?'

Crawford plunged on. 'But could Antoine—Mr Merrett, that is—have been a member of Mountain Rescue without being part of the climbing club?'

'Theoretically.'

'Could you tell me who to contact about its membership?'

'Me!' the man replied with a smile. 'I'm the membership secretary of that as well. And your man wasn't a member of it either. If he climbed, which I doubt, given what I saw of him on his TV commercials, it certainly wasn't as part of any organized group. He must have been freelance—as I said before.'

'I see.' Crawford decided to disengage. 'Well, thank you for your time. You've been most helpful.' He smiled.

The man snorted and turned away. Clearly he felt his time had been unjustifiably wasted.

2

WPC Williams had more luck.

'No. That was one of the odd things about him,' Zara Baradi said. 'He never usually said a word about hobbies or spare time. But now you mention it, I remember he did have climbing equipment down in the bottom of the shop. On the shelves.' She smiled at the older woman.

'And?' prompted Mrs Williams.

'I asked him one day when we were down there for something. "Spiderman must sleep here," I said. And he laughed. "Something like that," he said. "Something like that."'

'Nothing more?'

'Nothing more.' She frowned in thought, then relaxed. 'No. Like I say, he never said anything about what he did away from the shop.' She paused. 'Maybe Mrs Regan could help you there. But I'm afraid I can't.'

'And what did you think about it?'

The girl frowned. 'Nothing really. I mean, what was there to make of it? He never said anything more about it, and neither did I. It's up to him what he does in his own time.'

3

'That's all we need,' was Mason's response when Zara Baradi's 'information' was relayed to him. 'There's nothing more on that line.'

'Maybe.' Crawford hesitated.

Mason raised an eyebrow.

'Perhaps those different bank accounts were filled from robberies. He was maybe a burglar. He'd have been agile enough for that, by all accounts.'

Mason shook his head. 'I can just see the late and apparently unlamented Antoine swarming up the outside of buildings.' He laughed. 'Antoine, either as a Defender of the People or as some sort of cat-burglar, just does not fit.'

'Why not?' asked Crawford.

'Because we haven't had any proper cat-burglaries for years,' replied Mason. 'And besides, the basement had proper climbing kit. Remember the boots and that rope? You wouldn't use that sort of thing on a break-in.'

'Unless as a disguise,' Crawford suggested.

'And stick out like a sore thumb?' Mason was not amused at Crawford's persistence. 'Pull the other one.' He shook his head. 'No. I think that one's dead.'

'You know that story about hiding something in plain view? There just might be something there. I don't think we should dismiss it just yet.'

Mason shrugged. 'All right. But where does it leave us? It would be handy to know a bit more about friend Antoine, but where are we going to get more information? Besides—' he pulled the file towards him—'there's still the problem of that missing gardener to deal with. I think we should put out some publicity on him. Let's talk about that.'

But before they could, Mason's phone rang. A John Dundas was in the vestibule.

'John Dundas?' queried Mason, then remembered.

'Ah yes. Thanks. Crawford will come down and bring him up.'

John Dundas was carrying his stick. He had insisted on being taken home so that he could change first. There he had to explain what was going on, and his daughter, Susan, had insisted on accompanying him, much to his annoyance.

When they managed to convince the daughter that there was nothing sinister afoot, and she had retired to another room to wait, Mason and Crawford took Old John through the events of the Friday as he had seen them.

When it was over Mason commented wryly to Crawford, 'Well. He's of the old school! Punctilious!'

'Beyond belief,' replied Crawford.

'Still, better that way,' said Mason. 'But it doesn't take us any further. He left while Antoine was still at work.'

'But he did say he hadn't seen anyone else other than the gardener and the bridal party. Probably he was right. It wasn't a day to fetch others out.'

'And he knew that gardener's name. "Mr Strachan," indeed.'

'Had a good word for his workmanship, as well.'

'Mm. Good to hear that,' commented Mason. 'Still, let's call it a day, and beat the traffic.'

'Fine.' Crawford was agreeably surprised.

'Oh yes. Of course. I forgot. I've been busy all afternoon with Antoine's tax material. Opie brought it in. I have no way of knowing if it's accurate or not—not my problem. But at least the name's right. Or consistent. He's "Merrett' for tax purposes, while trading as "Antoine".'

'So what took up the time?'

'I was trying to get an estimate of what he was worth. The net profit's only part of it. The turnover and expenses are intriguing. By my reckoning the business doesn't explain that nice flat. The income and expenses match off to not much profit, and the expenses declared don't shelter enough expenditure to explain it either. He must have had some other source.'

4

'Cliffs,' Jane Mason said quietly as Mason finished jocularly telling her of the wild-goose chase Crawford and Williams had been on that afternoon.

'Cliffs?'

'Cliffs. There's quite a few people go climbing now on the cliffs. And there's some sort of artificial cliff in one of the country clubs. Dolly Madison was telling me about it.'

'Cliffs,' Mason agreed.

He went through to the kitchen to make tea. When he returned Jane had the TV on and the local news programme was just beginning. They watched it.

Mason shrugged as the brief report on the Antoine murder finished. Against stock footage of the Winter Garden, the sepulchral voice of one of their local reporters had intoned that the police were anxious to contact a Kevin Allan, a gardener at the Garden, 'in order to exclude him from their inquiries'. On a related matter, they were also still appealing for the person who had raised the alarm about the fire at Antoine's studio to get in touch.

'They might as well put up a flashing light—the police are wanting to arrest him,' Mason said, exasperated. 'That's no help at all, that way of putting things.'

Jane agreed. 'I wouldn't want to come forward if I heard my name on the TV like that. Even if I was innocent. It sounds just too ominous.'

'You read too many books.'

'Still, maybe the papers'll put it better. You wait and see.'

Mason stretched forward to pour another cup, and winced.

'It's the change in the weather,' observed Jane.

CHAPTER 8

FRIDAY

1

'Anthony Merrett. Antoine, we knew him as, but Merrett was his proper name. Yes, indeed. He was a member with us. An enthusiastic member, I may say. On the Management Committee as well.' The Secretary of the Greyhavens Health Club hesitated, then added apologetically, 'For a while, at least.' He went on in a more normal tone, 'He was convener of the Buildings Committee that saw to the addition of the climbing area and extended section to the gym. I was sorry to read of his death.' He was seated at the other side of a wide desk, fingers interlaced. 'I was expecting you to call.' He opened a drawer in the desk, pulled out some sheets of paper and slid one each to Mason and Crawford. 'I am afraid this is all that I can tell you officially about his association with us. At least, that's all that is in his file, though perhaps there are a couple of things I could add myself. And, of course, there are the Minutes of the Management Committee and of the Buildings Committee. Perhaps you should read what's there first.' He sat back and waited.

Mason scanned the sheet in his hand.

Anthony Merrett had been a member of the Health Club since it had opened four and a half years previously. Each time he had to be sent a reminder before paying his annual subscription, but had paid before the previous subscription had expired. On each occasion the subscription had been paid in cash. He had also taken out the extra subscription that entitled him to make use of the climbing apparatus.

Mason laid the sheet down on the desk.

'And you can add to this?' He tapped the sheet of paper.

The Secretary nodded. 'Not much. He was an agreeable member of the club, but detached. Semi-detached, I believe someone said of someone some time ago.'

'You knew he was a photographer?'

'Oh yes. We all knew that, though he never spoke of it. He was just keen on his climbing, and was very good at it.'

'Did he climb outwith the club? Out in the wild. In the hills.'

'He wasn't a mountain man, if that's what you mean. He was keen on cliff-climbing. It's become quite popular these last few years. I suppose it has the advantage that if you fall off, you're likely to drop into the sea. Much less messy.' He smiled.

'And not as cold.' Mason smiled back.

'Indeed. Merrett said as much to me one day when I had been watching him. He was quite remarkable, you know. His ability to go up a vertical face where you couldn't really see the hand and footholds from the ground . . . Remarkable. Quite remarkable.'

Mason nodded again. He leaned back. 'Is that all you can add?' He steepled his fingers in front of his nose. 'I got the impression that there was something more. You said he was involved in the administration. The Management Committee? A Buildings Committee?'

The Secretary leaned forward conspiratorially. 'Well, actually, there is something else.'

Mason leaned forward also. 'Yes?'

'I probably shouldn't say this, but you are the police.' He hesitated. Mason waited.

'It seems to me,' went on the other, 'that our late friend had some strange associates.'

Mason raised an eyebrow.

The man was suddenly flustered. 'I don't mean strange, strange. I mean strange, odd.' He glanced to either side, as if fearing someone were listening. 'Occasionally he would bring quite rough types to the Club. Sign them in as guests, and sit talking with them in the lounge—usually in a corner unit.'

'Nothing wrong with that,' observed Mason.

'Oh, I agree. I agree. It's just that . . . that they didn't seem his kind, as it were. More—' he let out a long breath and fluttered a delicate hand in the air. 'Business, but . . . More of the criminal fraternity, I would say. And as if he was doing deals.'

'Indeed?'

'There were oddities about it. Almost every person that he signed in was signed in using the same name.'

Mason raised both eyebrows.

'We have a book for signing-in guests. Every club does. But it was drawn to my attention that all Merrett's guests were surnamed Hector.'

'That sounds statistically improbable—unless it was the same person every time.'

'It wasn't. I paid attention to that.'

'May I ask why?'

The Secretary moved uncomfortably. He exhaled deeply. 'It just seemed odd. One of our staff on the front desk mentioned it to me—he had noticed—and after that I checked myself when I saw Merrett in the Club with a guest. They all were signed in as Hector. Different initials but all "Hector".'

'But he did sign in others?'

'Very few. And I noticed that—' the Secretary raised thumb and forefinger to his mouth and coughed apologetically—'that what I might describe as the less desirable types were all Hectors. If I could put it like that.'

'And I take it that no attempt was made to ask for identification from these people?'

'Hardly.' The man spread his hands.

'And no approach was made to Merrett for an explanation?'

'I did venture a comment once. I am afraid he told me to mind my own business.'

'Why did you not bring it to the attention of . . . I don't know. Presumably you have a Chairman of your Council?'

'I suppose so. I suppose so. But at the time Mr Merrett was engaged in important negotiations regarding the construction of the gym that I mentioned. He got extremely good prices.'

Mason looked at Crawford. Crawford nodded encouragingly, but did not take up the conversation. The Secretary glanced from one to the other.

He got to his feet. 'I am sorry. I probably should not have said all that. And I hope you will not tell anyone I said it to you. After all, the Management Committee might not like me talking to the police. But you are on a murder investigation, I believe.'

'Thank you,' said Mason. 'You are quite right. We are investigating Mr Merrett's murder. And you've been most helpful. We will try to avoid disclosing what you have said, but . . .' Mason shrugged. 'Now I wonder if you could show us this climbing wall, or whatever, that Merrett was so keen on.'

The Secretary led them out through a door into a large covered enclosure. 'I am afraid I must ask you to stay on the carpeted section,' he explained. 'Outdoor shoes can damage the wood.'

The point was immediately apparent. The floor was of sprung wood. But that was not what was most striking. The chamber was roofed and walled with glass. The outer walls and roof appeared to rest on two tall conical structures that reminded Mason of nothing so much as pictures he had seen of termite hills in Africa. About eight feet broad at the base, they tapered to about half that at the apex some thirty feet above. Their texture was of a sandy cement, with some cracks, crannies and indentations. A young man was slowly climbing his way up one of them. To one side a companion was taking the strain on a climbing rope that ran up to a rail on the apex of the tower, and then down to the climber. The climber was fumbling with a black pouch that hung from his belt. A puff of chalk drifted down as he grasped a small handhold.

The Secretary waved a hand in pride. Apart from the twin towers, there were three treadmills against the longest of the outer walls, their dials and lights shining against the gloom outside. Beside them were four sets of weight-training apparatus, benches and gleaming steel. Exercise bicycles stood beside the other outside wall.

Mason turned. The outer wall of the Health Club through which they had entered this cavern must have been built on, for the roof ran slightly up from the twin towers to the apex of the hall. The whole had been resurfaced to make an artificial cliff-face, with small projections and indentations.

As he took in the scene there came an audible curse from the climber. Mason turned to see him dangling from his rope, and his companion walking in towards the tower. The dangling man waved, and was lowered to the ground.

'Rather him than me,' Crawford murmured.

'So Merrett got this in place for you?' asked Mason.

'That's right.'

'Might I ask what it cost?'

'Some tens of thousands of pounds.'

'But Merrett got a good price for you?'

Crawford interrupted. 'You said something that

indicated to me that Merrett was a member of your Management Committee, but—I could have picked it up wrong—I got the impression that he did not serve out a full term on the Committee.'

The Secretary paused. He looked from Crawford to Mason and back. He sucked his teeth, and then spoke.

'There were some irregularities with the contracts. The matter was settled.'

'And had any of that to do with the various Messrs Hector?'

The Secretary shrugged.

'I wonder if we could see your guest book,' Mason asked thoughtfully.

'Certainly.'

Back in his office the Secretary sent for the guest book, and swiftly showed Crawford and Mason the entries he had mentioned. Crawford noted the dates.

'Any others spring to mind?' Mason asked.

'No,' replied the Secretary.

'Can I have a look?' asked Crawford. Before the other could answer, he spun the book to face himself, turned to the beginning, and began to run a finger down the names of the guests.

'I must say your Club seems in very good order,' Mason said. 'Are the fees high?'

The Secretary glanced quickly at Crawford, then gave his attention to Mason. 'We have various categories of membership. Are you interested? We have everything from a single person's membership, which entitles one to use the dining-room and lounge, through to a family membership that allows the entire family the full use of all the facilities, swimming pool, gymnasium and so on.'

'Have you a brochure? It might be interesting. I've thought for some time I should be getting more exercise.'

Crawford's fingers raced on, then slowed. He wrote something in his notebook.

'How large is the swimming pool? Might I see it?' Mason went on. 'We can leave my young friend here. He'll be quite safe.' Mason took the Secretary by the arm and turned him towards the door. 'We'll not be long,' he said to Crawford. 'Keep your hands off the silverware.'

The Secretary was not entirely certain that what was happening was proper. He glanced awkwardly back over his shoulder.

'I'm sure some of my colleagues would be keen to hear what the Club can offer,' Mason said smoothly.

The Secretary's attention was caught.

2

'Well,' said Mason expansively, leaning back in his chair. 'That's quite a find.'

Crawford closed his notebook, and nodded. 'It's too much to be a coincidence. You've got bank-books for what? Adams, Black, Silver.' He paused.

'Grey, Hector and White,' supplied Mason.

'And that Club has Antoine signing in A. Hector, B. Hector, G. Hector and S. Hector. Not to mention R. Hector and P. Hector.'

'And those others.'

'Who presumably are using their real names.'

'Quite.'

'But no addresses.'

'Quite.'

Crawford did not fall into the trap of explicitly drawing the conclusion.

Mason whistled tunelessly through his teeth and stared up at the ceiling for a few moments.

'But why would he have used Hector so often as a surname or alias for his friends and associates?'

Crawford shrugged.

'I bet it was a bit of bravado,' mused Mason. 'Cocking a snook. Two fingers to the establishment.' He got to his feet, and snorted a gentle laugh. 'I can go along with that a bit. But as to our business. If the bank-books link to the Hectors in the Club's Book, we now have to exclude that there actually is a Mr Hector Adams, Hector Black, Hector Grey and Hector Silver who knew Antoine. Or at least people willing to be signed in by Antoine under those names.'

He paused and went to the window. 'I wonder whether there is somewhere a similar signing-in for Hector Hector and Hector White.'

'And whether those are *their* real names,' Crawford commented dourly. 'Do you want all the clubs checked?'

Mason looked at him. 'No. I don't think I could justify the resources to do that.'

Crawford relaxed.

Mason smiled wolfishly. 'But at least Antoine/Merrett used his real name at the Club. And for his tax returns from Greyhavens, at least. We need to check in effect that the others are probably aliases.'

Crawford rose from his seat. 'Do we want to impound the Signing-In book?'

Mason raised an eyebrow. It was a good point. He pursed his lips. 'No. It's not likely to vanish. And if we took it someone might ask questions. Just get Paget to get someone to run the checks for Adams, etc.'

'Does it matter which they try first?'

'I wouldn't have thought so. But if they find a match they'll need to go out and check that off as well.'

'I suppose we'd better go beyond the District—but how far out?'

'The regional list would do for the . . .' Mason stopped, thought a moment, then started again. 'Start with the council-tax list, and the old Poll Tax listing, if that's still available. Then the local government electoral roll for the District and, say, one district further out from Greyhavens. After all, if there's some sort of criminal conspiracy going on between Antoine and any of them, I'd be most surprised if Antoine was working with someone living far out.'

'That Secretary said he had seen one or two— remember he checked—and they were business-types. Business, but . . .' He waved, mimicking the Secretary's gesture.

Mason agreed. 'So it's likely that Adams or whoever is either a property owner or a head of household. Or an elector.' He grinned again. 'Bet he votes Tory!'

'The consistent name letters still bother me,' mused Crawford. 'Why use A.A., B.B. and so on for the bank accounts, and yet sign in a series of guests as A. Hector, B. Hector and so on?'

'Presumably the A.A. and so on were simply convenient.' Mason leaned back and laughed. 'I heard some years ago a respected solicitor in this town say he had someone come in for advice off the street. It seems he was a criminal just out of the nick. Apparently he'd stashed away the proceeds of various robberies in bank accounts, but while serving time for them, he'd forgotten the names he'd used for the various accounts. Seems he could remember the branches, but not the names.'

'What had happened to the bank-books?'

'That wasn't clear.'

'So what was he wanting the solicitor to do?'

'He wanted him to write round asking about accounts that had not been operated on for the last *x* years, to see whether that would flush them out. He refused, of course.'

'So what would happen to the money?'

'Presumably the banks still have it, locked away in some inactive accounts list.'

'Can you open an account just like that?'

'Antoine managed. I suppose he might even have given his other names as referees, and quoted those banks as well.'

'All bank accounts,' mused Crawford suddenly. 'All bank accounts—no building societies.'

Mason looked at him, reviewing what he knew. 'I bet I can explain that,' he said. 'All the accounts are in small branches on the outskirts of Greyhavens. If he used building societies, he'd have to use the main streets. I mean there's almost no building society offices outside the centre, except ones linked to accountants' and lawyers' offices. He'd not want to use those. Too visible.'

'But someone like him would be known because of his TV advertising. The staff would recognize him.'

'Perhaps,' Mason replied. 'But passers-by wouldn't make much of it if they saw him once in a while going into a bank. Going into a main street building society would be too obvious to too many people.'

'I'm not convinced,' said Crawford. 'But I dare say we'll never know.'

He sat down at the other side of the desk, suddenly serious. 'There's one other thing occurs to me.'

Mason raised an eyebrow.

'Hiram Hector.'

'Well?'

'I'd lay money that that one's a big-shot Mason.'

'Yes,' Mason said slowly. 'I wondered about that too.'

'I wonder if Antoine was a Mason?'

Mason nodded, then looked up as Crawford began to laugh.

'I was going to say I didn't know a Mason to ask, then I remembered your name.'

Mason saw the funny side, then sobered and sighed. 'That's a real question, but not one I want to stir just now. But, tell you what. If it's a matter of building contracts—which was the inference of what the Secretary said about why Antoine left the Management Committee—then perhaps we should correlate with Alec Shepherd's investigation of those council contracts. And even if there's nothing there, it may be that he's got something somewhere about other scams. And those names would stick out like a sore thumb.'

He made a note on a pad, and put it into a desk drawer.

'Meantime,' he said, rising to his feet. 'I think we've had enough excitement for today.'

CHAPTER 9

SATURDAY

1

Crawford was at the table in the kitchen alcove buttering his toast when the phone rang. He twisted round to reach it and the sleeve of his bathrobe swept plate, toast, knife and butter to the floor. 'Damn!' he muttered as he picked up the phone.

'That's not a friendly-policeman-type expression.' It was Lucy's voice.

'Oh! Sorry. I didn't mean you. It's just that in getting the phone I've knocked the toast on the floor.'

'Clumsy!'

He waited. She had phoned him.

'You remember you invited me to the match today?' she said abruptly.

'Yes?'

'Can you get rid of your ticket?'

'Tickets.'

'Tickets, then. I thought . . .' She stopped, then started again. He smiled at a mental image. When she was off-balance she coloured up interestingly.

'Are you going to the match?' she asked in a less confident tone.

'Yes. Of course.'

'With company?'

'What kind of inquisition is this?'

'It's just that I've been told by my editor to go to the

match and write a piece about it—"Southern girl goes to first Greyhavens match"—that sort of thing.'

He waited, but she was silent.

'And?' he prompted.

'He's given me two stand tickets. Bang in the middle, apparently. Just below the Directors' box.'

'Oh.'

'And I wondered if you were going, if you'd like to use the other ticket—even if you've already got a ticket—tickets.' Her voice was small.

'I'd be pleased,' he replied casually. 'But, forgive my setting your editor right. You'd be far better behind the goal at the east end. That's where I always go.'

There was another pause. Then: 'Maybe we could compromise? One half down at the goal and the other up in the stand?' A chuckle lurked in her voice.

'Done.'

2

It was an evenly balanced match, but Greyhavens lost. Right at the end they gave away a penalty, and Rangers gratefully accepted the gift.

3

'I'm not sure I understand why people go and watch football,' she observed later, as they waited for their orders in the Pancake House.

'Is that what you're going to write? I don't know that your editor would want to see that. You'd certainly be flying in the face of a good many folk if you take that sort of line.'

The girl arrived with their plates as he finished.

Lucy shrugged. 'Maybe a little controversy is what he's looking for. He didn't give me a line to adopt.'

She put maple syrup on her stack of cakes.

'Even so.' He slathered butter on his top pancake and drowned it with maple syrup. Then he handed back the jug. 'Go on. They taste better half-drowned.'

She looked at his plate. 'Half?' she inquired sweetly, and then spoiled the effect by pouring more syrup on to her own plate.

'That's better,' he said. 'But what did you think?'

She sighed. 'I can see some attractions. But it was getting terribly cold towards the end. And what you'd do on a wet day, I just don't know.'

'That's all part of the experience.'

'And you can't see. Not really well. It'd be better to watch it on TV. That way, if you don't like what's on offer, you can always jump channels.' She smiled wickedly.

He took the point and grunted. 'That penalty should never have been given. Mostyn took a dive. All theatricals.'

'The goal was exciting.' She rubbed salt in the wound.

He ate in silence for a minute or so, and she followed suit.

'What other sports d'you like?'

'Other?' She thought a moment. 'I like watching tennis.'

He looked at her, and they spoke in unison. 'On TV.'

They finished the pancakes.

'Is that really your first time at a match?' he asked.

'Fifth amendment,' she smiled.

'Eh?'

'Isn't that what you say?' She held up a hand. 'I refuse to answer the question on the ground that it may incriminate me. McCarthy and all that.'

'I've news for you. The US Constitution doesn't apply over here.'

'But something similar does. You can't force someone to answer a question.'

'Yeah. That's right.' He sounded flat.

'Without meaning to pry into anything current, d'you find that a problem?'

'Without saying anything about anything—yes.' He swirled his tea in the cup and studied it. 'There are times when it would be useful to be able to insist on an answer.'

'Even a misleading one?'

He put the cup down and looked at a couple in the corner. 'Even a misleading one. Then at least you've got something to check. And if it is misleading you can use it to get somewhere. Challenge them, you know.'

'And without that?'

'Without that there are times you feel you're in a complete fog.'

She nodded sympathetically. 'I feel like that sometimes, too.' She put her head on one side as he shifted uneasily. 'I repeat, I'm not wanting any hints on current events. I'm talking other times, other stories. Sometimes you just don't know where to go. You know there's something, but not where to get through to it.

He straightened, and grinned boyishly. 'I thought you journalists just printed whatever you think you can get away with. Accuracy unimportant, just so long as the libel writ doesn't arrive. You know.'

She made a face. Then she sighed deeply. 'Yes. I suppose that's justified in some cases.'

He leaned forward. 'What was that rule I read of in the Watergate book? "Get two to say it and you can print"?'

She waggled a finger at him. 'Close, but not close enough. Two independent sources and you can print. That's the rule.'

'You could still make mistakes with that.'

She nodded. 'Yeah. That's why it's not the usual rule we would rely on. You check your story every-which-way-from-Friday before you go to print. If there's any possibility of error.'

'Every what?'

She ignored the question. 'It's only an emergency rule. You only do it if it's something absolutely important—as where there might be a defamation writ nailed to the door if you get it wrong.'

'But in other instances you just rely on less.'

She nodded.

'And it's your head on the block?'

'Umm.' She waggled her head to one side and the other. 'Not quite. It's ultimately the responsibility of the Editor. You draw his attention to things and he decides.'

'And if you tell him wrong? I mean, he's got to rely pretty much on what you say.'

She shrugged. 'Newspaper people aren't often fired for that sort of reason. More likely for drinking, missing stories or fiddling expenses too blatantly.'

'Or the company gets in a mess.'

'Quite.'

'Ever been fired?'

'Once.' She paused. 'And exactly as you said. The company was trying to cut costs, so they did without my measly salary as an economy.'

'Not nice.'

'Not nice. Particularly as I could see it coming.'

'So why stay around for it?'

'Redundancy pay. It allowed me to take those weeks off to try to write the book.'

'Did that ever appear?'

She shook her head. 'If you recall, circumstances rather knocked inspiration on the head.'

He grinned.

'So now you write so-called fact instead.' He paused. 'We cut out all the reports and put them in the file as well as our own data.'

'Why?' She was surprised.

'You folk go around and ferret out things just as we do. You talk to the neighbours and friends. You interview the milkman, even. And sometimes, there's just a chance that you turn up something we don't have.'

'I thought we agreed that Antoine was off-limits,' she said very seriously.

'It is. It is. I'm not changing that, even if you were willing to talk, which I doubt. What is it? Protecting confidentiality of sources? Isn't that the usual way journalists put it?'

'I think we might disagree about that,' she replied. 'But it is terribly important. If people don't think you'll keep their identities secret, they'll not tell you things.'

'That doesn't apply from where I'm sitting. People make statements all the time. And they know it's part of the investigation. And that they may have to stand up in court and go through it all again for the benefit of a jury.'

She leaned forward earnestly. 'But there must be times when you have to promise secrecy.'

'Not in that way. We might say that if possible we will seek independent confirmation of something with the result that the first source does not have to be disclosed. But that's as far as I would go.'

'And Mason?'

Crawford shrugged.

She sat up straight, clearly considered what she was going to say next, and said it.

'I don't want an answer to this. But. Have you considered a link between your murders and the council inquiries that are being conducted by Chief Inspector Shepherd?'

Crawford sat still.

'Oh dear.' She slumped in her chair. 'I oughtn't to have said that. I'm sorry.'

He smiled thinly, paused, then spoke. 'Let's go back to the first agreement. These things are off-limits.'

She felt behind her for her coat.

'I was wondering if you'd fancy seeing a film tonight,' he said, getting up and holding the coat for her.

She shook her head. 'I'd love to. But I'd better get something written while it's still fresh in my mind.'

CHAPTER 10

MONDAY

1

'I need to talk to you.' Lucy Gottman had been insistent, and Ian Crawford reluctantly agreed to meet her for lunch close to police headquarters. His reluctance lay not in meeting Lucy—that was an increasing pleasure—but in the middle of the day he was very busy. Besides, they had been together only a couple of days earlier.

'How about the Captain's Cabin at six or six-thirty?' he had offered at first.

'Before that would be better.'

He wondered at that. They got on well together, but her tone was flat and yet urgent. 'I'm very busy,' he said.

'So am I. But I need to see you about something. Is lunch-time possible? It wouldn't take long.'

'How about evening?'

'I'm busy.'

Ah, he thought. It must be business. Was it to do with the Antoine affair? Or was there something else she wanted to raise? A vision of Mason's lifted eyebrow formed in his mind. Firmly he pushed it away. Alan Mason could hunt his own spectres and fears.

The evening would have suited him better, but she had ruled that out. She was busy—as if he weren't!

'I need to see you about something, and either it's lunch-time, or not.'

'Can't it wait?'

'Trust me.' He could hear a smile in her voice. She had perceived his weakening.

'All right. Captain's Cabin at half twelve.'

2

She was waiting at a corner table when he appeared.

'What'll you have?' he asked.

'We're going dutch on this,' she responded.

He was agreeable. They had got to an easy enough friendship for neither to take such an arrangement amiss. Besides, each knew the other was not earning so much as to make treating a regular occurrence.

'Well?'

'I'm for the broccoli lasagna,' she replied, speaking to the waitress who had materialized at their side.

Crawford nodded. 'Me too. Drink?'

'Just a Coke.'

'Two Cokes.' The waitress went off.

Crawford shrugged his coat over the back of his chair, and settled.

'What's ado?'

'A problem,' she sighed. 'I'm very sorry, and I hope you won't be mad!'

'That sounds promising.'

She picked up a large envelope from beside her chair. 'It's this.' She held the envelope in her hands and looked carefully at him. 'You remember the Rangers' penalty on Saturday?'

'Could I forget it?' He rolled his eyes to heaven. That penalty had sunk Greyhavens' chances for the season.

She nodded sympathetically. 'Yes. But there's this as well.' She drew a photograph part way out of the envelope, then pushed it back in. 'Bill Sheffield was at the match.'

'Bill?'

'He's the senior photographer at the *Gazette* and he's daft on football.'

'Oh yeah. I saw him. I know Willie Sheffield. He does those marvellous action photos?'

'The same.'

'Since when was he called Bill?'

'He's always called Bill round the office.' She frowned.

'Is he now? He's always Willie Sheffield to me, that is, after I grew up.'

'Oh! I'm glad you know him. Maybe that'll make this easier.'

'So?'

'Well, you remember, I thought that penalty was good. It was well taken wasn't it? It rocketed into the net.'

Crawford shook his head in demurral.

The girl pulled the photo out of the envelope and laid it on the table in front of him. 'Bill—I mean Willie—is going to enter this in a national competition.'

The picture was a beauty, glossy fine-grain black and white. It showed a small group of football spectators, men and boys. In the front row in the middle were a man and a girl. The men all looked as though they had just witnessed an act of high tragedy. The boys had either the same expression as the men, or were turning their faces to their fathers for reassurance or guidance. The girl was cheering.

'He's going to call it "Odd Girl Out".'

Crawford picked the photograph up. 'I don't remember seeing him,' he commented.

'It's a blow-up. Bill was using a long focus, but when he saw the contacts he blew up this bit as well. The whole print takes in the lot, goalkeeper and all. He came and showed me. The full picture showed the goalie and the net, but there was this as well. He enlarged it,' she explained. 'He thinks this is a shot to stick into this competition. I thought you ought to see it first,' she added in a small voice.

The photo lay on the table in front of him. He and the others looked like fools, hypnotized, inert with shock. He remembered the feeling. It had been the closing minutes of the game. A draw would have done. There had been no score. First there had been disbelief at the referee's decision that the tackle had been a foul. The other defenders had protested—perhaps too much. But the ref had not been moved, and all behind the goal had succumbed to some sort of slow horror. Inexorable and slow, the events took their course from that heavy tackle. The ball had been placed. Munro had run up. The keeper had flung himself valiantly, and had picked the right side. He had almost succeeded—but the ball caromed from the forearm, past him and off the upright into the net. And Greyhavens was out of contention.

Beside him Lucy had cheered!

He swallowed a couple of times and made the best of a bad job. 'Maybe you could get me one or two of them?' His tone was conspiratorial.

'Ordinary members of the public can order through the down-town office in St Martin's Square.' She paused, then relaxed. 'But sometimes special arrangements can be made. I was just worried that you'd be annoyed.'

He laughed. 'What d'you want me to do? Bar Willie from sending it in? It's a good shot.'

'You won't mind?'

'Fat chance Willie would pay any attention to me. Not on a professional matter, any more than I'd listen to him.' He paused and looked at her. 'But how about you? If you're worried about it, I'll talk to him.'

'You just said he'd pay no attention to you.'

Crawford smiled. 'Well, you know what it's like. There are some ties. He moved into a house across the lane from my folks. I grew up with his son. We were in and out of each other's houses regularly. We used to play kypie together in junior school, raid the apple trees from the back lane—generally be young hooligans together.'

'Kypie?'

Crawford drew himself up and pretended solemnity. 'Sorry. I forgot you're from the south. I ought to have said marbles.' He paused and his face grew solemn. 'I haven't heard of Malcolm for ages. He went south and stopped writing anyone back here—even his folks.'

'That's sad.'

Crawford nodded. 'I think Willie feels it. That's why I never ask if he's heard from him.'

He gave his shoulders a slight shake, dismissing the unwelcome train of thought. 'Actually, if you're upset by the prospect of that going on public display or anything—' he tapped the photo with a finger—'I think Willie could be persuaded—even by you. The old man's got a kindly streak. Probably that's why he showed you it. To give you the chance.'

She relaxed. 'Oh, I don't mind.' She picked up the photo and turned it round to look at it. 'It's rather good. It's just I was worried what you might think. Mason seems so stern sometimes.'

Crawford hadn't thought of that. 'Mm. There's a point.' He hesitated. 'Still, maybe.' He took the photo back, scrutinized it, then gave it back. 'No. I think that he'd not object. Not if it wins!' He chuckled.

When Crawford walked across the open area in front of Headquarters he saw Mason standing at his window looking down at him. There was another of the hated yellow notes on his desk. He grimaced and set off for Mason's office.

'I am sorry, sir. I do apologize.' Crawford stood stiffly to attention.

'I quite realize that it is in the interests of the Force to keep good relations with the local Press, but you will not leave this building without either my permission, or if for some reason that cannot be obtained in time, without leaving a phone number. And it was quite inexcusable not to have taken your bleeper.' Mason was as angry as Crawford had seen him for some time.

'I did not suggest any such reason, sir. It was an error, which I will not repeat.'

Mason glared at him, then suddenly smiled. 'I'm sorry,' he said. 'I was young once. But I'll tell you why I am angry. The CC came in to ask how things were going, and I sent for you, and the CC worked out that I didn't know where you were. So—' Mason wagged a finger—'you'd better watch your step. You don't want the Boss thinking you weren't worth your promotion.'

'No, sir.'

'And if he happens to ask you in the corridor, for heaven's sake remember that you went out for several purposes—a pair of shoes, or to collect laundry, or something. With Miss Gottman so far down the list that you never get there. And you can indicate that I chewed you out about it.'

Crawford was starting to agree when the phone rang. The message was short and to the point. 'You're sure?' Mason listened a few more moments, and the put the phone down.

'Kevin Allan is on the bus coming in the south road. It seems he's been at the Standing Inn, just short of Darroch. Find out when it's due—he left about half an hour ago—and get someone over to keep an eye on his house. You and I'll go down and meet the bus. He'll most likely come right through to the bus station because he'd easiest collect the 15 from there. But if he's trying to get away, he'll get off earlier and go roundabout to home and pick up whatever he's needing.'

'How long have we got?' Crawford asked.

Mason looked at his watch, then phoned the bus station. 'About an hour and a half,' he said. 'Maybe more. It seems it's the first bus they've managed to get along the south side of the valley since last week, and there are places that aren't too good yet.'

There was a knock at the door. It was Inspector Paget, with a clipboard in his hand.

'I've got an almost zero on that question you left on Friday,' he said to them both.

'Almost?'

Paget looked at his list. 'No Adamses. Three Brian Blacks, one is away on holiday and one is a father and son group, schoolteacher and first year University. Two Hector Greys. One's off-shore on the oil-rigs and has been for a fortnight—due back tonight according to his wife.'

'And the other?'

'In the Old Folk's home down beside the Winter Garden. He's in his eighties.'

'Ah well,' said Mason. 'Thanks for trying.'

'D'ye want me to go further afield? It's just a matter of a few buttons once we're linked in.'

Mason turned to Crawford, who shook his head. He turned back to Paget. 'Not just yet. There's something else we've to go over first. But thanks. It's a help.'

'Buttons!' Mason commented to Crawford once Paget had gone. 'I'm sure basically he thinks it's some form of higher magic.'

3

'That's him, I bet.' Crawford cocked a finger and pointed at the rangy figure getting off the bus. He started forward, but paused as Mason gripped his elbow.

'Wait,' said the older man quietly.

Crawford turned to his boss, a question in his eyes.

Mason shrugged. 'I'm sure you're right. He's the only one fitting the description coming off that bus. But it just might be that the one we want got off earlier and didn't go home yet. Besides—' he turned slightly to have another sight of the man now waiting for the luggage compartment of the bus to be opened—'this one interests me. He's very well in command of himself. Let's see where he goes.'

Apparently chatting gently together, the two of them happened to follow Kevin Allan as he crossed the road and waited at a bus stop.

To Mason's surprise, Allan did not board the 15 that came along quite soon. That was the bus that went along Kevin Allan's street. Instead he got on the 19 that came along immediately behind it.

Crawford and Mason boarded the 19 as well, and sat chatting as it went on its winding trip down to the Park.

There Allan got off the bus, and set off at a smart pace, heading towards the Orangerie. Mason and Crawford followed, more slowly.

Inside, there was no sign of Allan. Mason went first to the gardeners' cubbyhole across the rustic bridge, and then led the way up the small connecting house to the service rooms at the rear of the building. Again there was no sign of their quarry.

'Hell,' said Mason shortly. 'There's a back way out, isn't there?'

'Yes,' said Crawford, and set off, past the huge geraniums that covered the rear wall, and through into the new area. Mason followed.

Albert Strachan was working in the area, bedding some miniature bushes. He straightened as the two came through.

'Has Allan gone through here?' asked Crawford, pointing to the external door.

'No,' Albert responded. 'I've not seen him since that day I was telling you about.' He scratched his head. 'Have you seen him?'

'Is there somewhere else here that he could be?' asked Mason.

'Unless he's gone up to see Webster.'

'Webster?'

'The Supervisor. He's got an office above the potting sheds. I saw him come in earlier on.'

'Oh yes. Webster. How do we get up there?'

'There's a stair at the rear, behind the false wall on the right in the sheds.'

This time Mason led the way, but at a more sedate pace.

They found Kevin Allan sitting with his head in his hands. Webster was prone on the floor in front of him.

As the two men came into the room Webster groaned and moved slightly. Allan made to get up and then slumped down into the chair once more.

'What's going on?' asked Mason.

Allan glanced up at him. 'What's it to you?' he responded listlessly. Then his eyes narrowed. 'I wondered if you two were following me.'

'Did you do this?' Mason pointed at Webster who, helped by Crawford, struggled to a sitting position as he spoke, his hand to his jaw.

'What if I did?'

'I am a police officer. Assault is a crime.'

'Crime, is it?' Allan's lip curled and he sat straighter. 'Am I a criminal now?'

'Are you Kevin Allan?' Mason asked.

The other nodded once.

'In that case I must ask you to accompany me. I have

questions for you.' He turned to Webster. 'We seem to have arrived marginally late,' he commented. 'Perhaps you would come with us as well?' His tone gutted the use of the question form.

4

'So you might just have fallen down as we were coming up the stairs? Pull the other one! Why would Kevin Allan come back into town, get on a bus and come all the way down here to hit you almost as soon as he saw you?' Mason was curt.

The mane of silver hair shook slowly. 'I have nothing to say,' responded Webster.

Mason stared at him, then jerked his head at Crawford and went and stood in a corner.

'We should be doing him for assault,' said Crawford gently. 'But unless you are willing to tell us what happened, we've got no case that would stand up in court.'

Webster shrugged. His hand went again to his jaw-line, and gently caressed it. 'I've got nothing to say,' he said again. 'Nothing to say. Let me go away!' He looked from one to the other, almost pleadingly, Mason thought.

'We could do you for failing to assist a policeman in the execution of his duty.' Mason came forward again.

Webster shrugged once more. 'Too bad.' He massaged one thumb with the other.

Mason heaved a deep sigh. 'You'd better go,' he said disgustedly. 'We've got other things to spend our time on.'

'Is Kevin away home as well?' asked Webster, getting to his feet.

Mason cocked his head. 'Why should that concern you?' he asked in some surprise. 'If you're worried he may have another go at you—tell us what went on this afternoon.'

'None of your business.'

'If you're planning something . . .' Crawford's voice trailed off.

Mason turned to him, then turned back to Webster.

'I second that,' he stated. 'If it was something like—let's see. "He took you by surprise, but this time you're going to get your retaliation in first." Let me warn you, if anything happens to Kevin Allan at your hands, I will throw the book at you.'

Webster's lip twisted. He glanced from Mason to Crawford and back. 'Can I go?' he asked.

Mason stared at him. There was something lurking at the back of the man's eyes. He was not the blustering character who had demanded they allow the re-opening of the Winter Garden for wedding photography. Whence had the change come?

Allan was equally difficult.

He sat on the flimsy wooden chair, facing Mason across the government issue table, his elbows tucked to his waist and his hands clenched under his chin. He rocked backwards and forwards, blinking his eyes slowly.

'I want you to tell me what happened that afternoon.'

'What afternoon?'

'Friday afternoon.'

'I was up on the High Top.'

Mason's hand slammed down on the table-top.

'I told you before. Not last Friday. The Friday before. The last Friday you were at work in the Orangerie. You are Kevin Allan. You are a widower and you work at the Orangerie as an employee of the Council, are you not?'

'I am all that.'

'You were there last Friday—a week ago—when Antoine, the photographer, was taking pictures of a wedding party.'

Allan shook his head.

'Your fellow employee says you were.'

'Ah, Albert. Albert, the Bulbul Ameer.' A smile flicked across Allan's face as he recollected the old song.

'He says you were there,' said Crawford, as Mason glanced at him in exasperation.

'He's wrong,' came the reply, almost whispered.

'So where were you?'

'Round the back. Round the back. As soon as I saw him coming in, I left.'

'Why?'

Allan straightened. He looked shrewdly at first Mason and then Crawford. 'Couldn't stand the man,' he said abruptly and folded himself up again.

'You must have a reason.'

'Must I?' This time the reply was whispered. Mason leaned forward, as did Crawford, to hear. 'Must I have a reason, now.' Allan straightened again, and once more looked first at one, then at the other of the interrogators. 'Why must I have a reason for doing anything? Does God have a reason for what he does? If he does, I can't see it. He makes lovely scenery. But people?' He shook his head.

'Where have you been for the last few days?' Crawford asked quietly.

Kevin smiled bleakly. 'I come from going up and down upon the earth.'

'What does that mean exactly?' queried Mason. 'You had climbing kit with you. Have you been into the hills?'

'And you a detective,' sighed Allan. 'Of course that's where I've been. I said I was up on the High Top. Didn't you see me get off the valley bus? You were following me. You saw that. Why ask?'

'You have been in the mountains. I thought anything above the valley was all drifted up.'

'The drove road above the Inn is free. It's windcleared almost always.'

'We have been looking for you.'

Allan frowned. 'So why did you come to that bus? That couldn't have been an accident.' He paused, then shot to his feet and leaned across the table. 'Was it Bailey?'

'I don't know that name,' said Mason smoothly.

'The Standing Inn. That's where I've been. Did they phone and tip you off? That I was coming back into town?'

'We were looking for you.' Mason gestured to Allan to sit, and he did so. 'You must have expected that. The news that Antoine was found dead in the Orangerie was well broadcast, and yet you chose to go away. You must have realized that we would want to speak to you.'

'I had to go think.'

'What about?'

'Things.' Allan folded himself again and shut his eyes, turning his head on one side.

Mason stared at him, then asked, 'What things?'

'Things.'

'You must have realized that looks very suspicious to someone investigating a murder.'

Allan shrugged.

Mason pounced. 'From which I deduce that you knew that it was a murder. Yet there was nothing in the press or broadcasting before you left that said that. The most that was said was that there was a body believed to be that of the photographer Antoine.'

Allan glanced sideways at Crawford, and breathed deeply twice. 'I suppose if that's how it looks, that's how it looks. But I was wanting to get into the hills to think out a few things. It's just a co-in-cidence.' He dragged the last word out, and smiled crookedly.

'What did you do before you were employed by the District?' Mason asked suddenly.

'Before the Winter Garden?'

Mason nodded.

'I was with the Dustrict cleansing. Dust—rick. Joke,' snorted Allan.

'And before that?'

'Unemployed.'

'And before that?'

'Why?'

Mason spread his hands in a low-key shrug.

'Helping the Queen.'

'What for?'

Allan paused. 'Oh, I see. You think I mean I was a guest of Her Majesty. No. I was with the Army. Fifteen years.'

'How did you get the Council job?'

'Merit.'

'How long have you been with the Council?'

Allan shrugged. 'A few years. The employment record at the Council offices would show exactly.'

'Before your wife died?'

Allan stiffened, then nodded.

'Did you know Antoine, the photographer.'

Allan made a face. 'Him!' he said in deep disgust. 'Of course I knew him. He was forever prancing about in the Winter Garden.'

'So you left when you saw him coming in.'

'That's what I said.'

They got no further with Kevin Allan. They let him go with an instruction not to leave town, and went back to Mason's office.

Mason shrugged as he interpreted Crawford's expression. 'I know. I know. We can't enforce it, but it's sometimes useful to say things like that, just in case.'

Crawford raised a shoulder. 'Maybe,' he replied. 'But not in that case, I'd say.'

Mason raised his eyebrows.

'I think he's a lot too intelligent to fall for that.' He

paused, then gathered pace. 'I'd say he's pretty intelligent. And I wonder why he's in a job like that. There must be lots of other things he could do.'

Mason raised his hands and looked at them. 'Maybe,' he countered. 'But I could see attractions in spending your days growing beautiful plants, the way they do down there. It's a pretty skilled job.'

'You said nothing about the other body.'

'Neither I did.' Mason's tone was low.

Crawford waited.

'I want someone in plain clothes to go to Allan's neighbourhood, with a copy of the photograph. Not to Allan. Nor to anyone that seems a close friend. They'll have to chat a little.'

Crawford put his head on one side. He was puzzled.

Mason got to his feet, and stuck his hands deep in his pockets. He stretched himself. Crawford knew the signs. Mason did not like what he was about to say. He waited.

'Did you see Allan in profile?' Mason asked and went to his window, looking out and down. Crawford did not reply.

Mason swung abruptly. 'I want you to find out anything you can about Allan's time "helping the Queen".'

Crawford added instruction to instruction, and unstated element to unstated element. His stomach congealed.

Mason turned back. 'I don't think he'll do anything silly.' He tapped a finger on the desk, came to a decision, and picked up the phone.

Crawford made to leave, but Mason wagged a hand at him. 'While you were on your extended lunch-break, I arranged that we'd go see Alec Shepherd.' He gave his attention to the phone.

'Alec. Sorry. Something came up. Did Alice get my message to you? Good. Any chance we can come along now?'

He put the phone down.

5

Alexander Shepherd was pleased to see them. They sat at the conference table at the side of his office, which had a few files heaped at one end of it.

'Thanks for the list,' he said. 'There is a match with some of the names.'

'Let me guess,' responded Mason. 'Black and Grey.'

Shepherd nodded, and looked quizzically at Mason. 'We do not have a Hector or an Adams.'

'So the colour names fit one type of operation—the one you're putting together.'

'Seems so. We have a Blue and a White as well that might fit as well in a similar range. You say you have a Green?'

'That could be very interesting,' replied Mason. 'We seem to have a dead Green, and those other names I gave you come from bank-books found in his flat.' He saw Crawford's puzzlement. 'Remember, Ian? George Green is the name of the Council-tax payer for Antoine's flat.'

'Ah!'

'Excellent,' said Shepherd, rising to his feet. 'That would fit very nicely. Green just might be the banker.'

'And in that case he may have died because of irregularities in his accounts.' Mason laughed wryly. 'That's quite a good way of making sure your accountant stays in line.'

'Indeed.'

'It occurs to me . . .' interjected Crawford, then realized he had interrupted.

'Go on,' encouraged Shepherd, turning to him.

Crawford looked to Mason for guidance, who nodded.

'It was just that what you're saying sounds a little like the theory about Baxter.'

'Baxter?' Shepherd was uncertain.

'Malcolm Baxter. Middle-ranker. Died under odd circumstances four/five years ago,' explained Mason. 'Were you involved?' he asked Crawford.

'That Baxter.' Shepherd was interested.

'It was the first case I was really on.'

Mason took up the story. 'Baxter was in the reset business, and not above providing his own materials from building sites and anywhere he could get things. Done quite well.'

'That's right,' said Shepherd. 'He was run down on the dual carriageway. He had been drinking.'

Mason held up a hand. 'It all seemed a bit too convenient. His mistress managed to get a declarator of marriage and therefore got the house and most of the bank accounts, and she's now shacked up with old Bernie.'

'I see your point, there,' responded Shepherd. He turned to Crawford. 'But how does that relate to my problem?'

Crawford swallowed, and pressed on. 'It's just that I remember there was an opinion at one stage that Baxter had been removed, not to let his boss get his girlfriend, but as a matter of discipline.'

'That's right,' said Mason. 'There was such a hypothesis. So? Where's the connection in this lot?'

'Building thefts. And Reginald Opie.'

The room went silent.

'Opie was the solicitor for Baxter, and for Bernie. He got the declarator through the Court of Session. He's also Antoine's solicitor.'

After a few more seconds Mason grunted a suppressed laugh. 'No. No. That's just a bit too tenuous. After all, there's a connection between you, Baxter and Antoine. You all know Opie.'

'But I came on the scene afterwards, and the others are—were—clients of Opie. What I meant was really just that if you were thinking that Antoine's death was a matter of discipline, there was perhaps a parallel to a previous case. It was backing up what you said.'

'I know. I know,' said Mason placatingly.

'But the laddie's maybe not foolish,' said Shepherd slowly. 'The roots of what I have go very far back. It might just all tie up together.'

Mason shrugged. 'What we think we can offer is a set of dates and a place of meeting for Mr Green and a Hector Adams, a Hector Black, a Hector Grey and a Hector Silver.'

'Hector?' Shepherd was wary.

'Hector!' affirmed Mason. 'That was why someone was drawn to note the peculiarity. All of them were named "Hector", but A. Hector, B. Hector and so on. We reckon the Hector was common, and A, B indicate Adams, Black.'

'Ah,' Shepherd became animated. 'Someone who might recognize a few photos?'

'Doubt it, but it may be worth a try. But in any case the dates might tie up with something else you've got.'

CHAPTER 11

TUESDAY

Mason sat quietly as Crawford reported. The photograph had been recognized. Two of the neighbours had also passed on some local gossip. Allan's Army record was summarized on the sheet of paper Crawford had given him.

'Anything else?' Mason asked.

'Only that Reginald Opie wants to see you. Something about the Antoine estate.'

'He can wait.'

'Oh yes. There's also Mrs Regan. She's back home and phoned. She's willing to come in for interview.'

'Fine. Schedule that for early afternoon, if you can. Which failing, you'll have to go out with WPC Williams again.' Mason smiled.

Grim-faced, Mason went back to see Alex Shepherd, and they conferred. Then the two went to see their superior officer, files in hand.

'You think that this man does not know his son's dead, although there is a possible hypothesis that he killed Antoine and fired the Studio to mislead the inevitable inquiry,' Cochrane summed matters up.

'That's it, sir.'

'And you want to delay getting him to identify the body.'

'Yes.'

Cochrane looked bleakly at Mason. 'The problem is that you are unconvinced that he is the murderer.'

'But I think he knows who is.'

'Who is?'

'I am not quite sure, but there is a possibility of overlap with other inquiries going on within the department. If I act on what I've got, it just might upset what Alec's getting close to.'

'And you agree with that?' The question was to Shepherd, who nodded.

'Someone once said that the simplest explanation was always the right one.' Cochrane was doubtful.

'William of Occam said that the right explanation is the simplest one that fitted all the facts,' Mason corrected him.

Cochrane looked carefully at him. 'So what does the simple "Allan is the murderer" not fit? You tell me that neighbours say that the photograph is of Allan's son. You also tell me they say there was a Godalmighty row when the son dropped out of University to go photographing with this Antoine. And that Allan was an Army man, a sergeant in Northern Ireland. He'd have been trained in that sort of *modus operandi*, to coin a phrase.'

'It's just a feeling, sir. I think he's come back to look for his son. If he had killed Antoine, he'd not come back. I think he knows who did the Antoine killing, but is back trying to retrieve his son. And, like I say, we—Alec and I—think our cases are interconnected.'

Cochrane glanced at Shepherd, who nodded assent.

Cochrane made up his mind. 'All right. You can have till Thursday. Beyond that I think you have to reel him in and tell him—if he doesn't find out about the extra body before then. If that happens, then if you're right, he'll maybe come to us unasked. But from what you say, he's more likely to visit the killer. And then what? Might we have another murder on our hands?'

'How about Friday?' Mason asked, ignoring the other

questions Cochrane had framed. 'Thursday is Christmas Day.'

'Thursday,' repeated Cochrane. 'Crime takes no holidays. And I must say, I think you're wrong. It sounds more likely to me that Allan did Antoine.'

'Phew,' he remarked to Shepherd as they went back to their offices. 'I've not seen him like that for ages. You'd think an extra day at Christmas would not matter.'

'I should have warned you,' Shepherd replied. 'His daughter's just got engaged, and he's less than pleased about it.'

Mason raised an eyebrow.

'She went on holiday to Spain.'

Mason's brain caught up with his ears. 'Not Myrtle!' He laughed. The plain Myrtle Cochrane had been the object of cruel jokes for years.

Shepherd was serious. 'Myrtle. She's selling her flat and moving out there. They say he's a croupier.'

Mason stopped short in astonishment. Shepherd took his arm. 'Come on,' he said. 'We've got a wee bit of a breathing space on your problem, and maybe a lever on mine.'

Mason grunted. 'A croupier!'

When he got back to his office, Reginald Opie was waiting for him.

'I must ask for the return of those various documents,' said Opie smoothly.

'We're not finished with them.'

'But Antoine's sister is coming up, and I must have the documentation in order properly to advise her.'

'You have the receipts.'

'They are not entirely helpful.'

'You know what you provided.'

'But not the detail. And there are items removed from the flat that require scrutiny.'

'Indeed?'

'Numerous bank-books are listed, for example.'

'Eight.'

'I need to know what the amounts on deposit are. To give Mrs Matthews some idea of the size of the estate.'

'There were considerable sums in them,' stated Mason. 'But I think you have a further difficulty there.'

Opie looked his question.

'I am afraid that there is no evidence that any of these books were actually Antoine's. They are all in different names.'

Opie was astonished, then calculating. 'You mean we would have problems in establishing that they are part of the estate?'

'Precisely.'

Opie drew himself up. 'That would be a problem for the executor, soluble by the employment of a component graphologist. But it is no reason for you to retain the material.'

'I am sorry. I cannot let you have the material as yet. Nor have I the resources over the Christmas period to provide more detail. You will have to wait a little time.'

Opie's eyes narrowed. 'Do I deduce that you hope to report progress in this distressing matter?'

'Of course I hope to report progress,' said Mason blandly. 'But I would not forecast a timetable for it. There are too many awful warnings against that course of action.'

Opie laughed. 'Ah! Do you think our respected Chancellor of the Exchequer will survive?'

'Look, I am sorry. I cannot help you now. You'll just

have to muddle through for a few days. Tell her things are stuck because of the police investigation. That there are important matters afoot. After all, it is a murder we are investigating. How's she taking it, by the way?'

Opie smiled and gestured briefly. 'I have the impression she couldn't care less about Antoine. But the question of the estate is exercising her greatly.'

'The name's not Robinson, is it?' Mason suddenly asked.

'As a matter of fact it is. How do you get there? Is there information in the stuff you seized?'

'You may have an interesting executry on your hands,' replied Mason, smiling enigmatically.

'If her holiday's done her any good, she must have been in a right mess before she went,' Crawford commented as he and WPC Williams left the Regan house.

Williams agreed.

'Takes us little further,' Crawford went on. 'She didn't know this Russell's full name either, but he obviously had enough authority to tell her what to do. He did the printing and sent her off to the Brightside Hotel.'

'Tell you what struck me,' said WPC Williams. 'She didn't say that this Russell person was affected in any way by Antoine's disappearance. I wonder if he expected it. Or if it happened before. Or even often.'

Crawford could have kicked himself. He had not noticed those points himself. But there was no way they could return to the weeping woman and reopen the question. Not that day, at least.

He drove somewhat abstractedly, disturbed by Williams's comment. At the roundabout at the top of the road he barely missed a large blue Jaguar making full use of its right of way. It was as they parked at Headquarters that his subconscious categorized the glimpse he had had of the Jaguar's driver. It might have been Webster.

He went off to run a check through the car registration computer.

CHAPTER 12

WEDNESDAY/THURSDAY

1

'It was the night before Christmas, and all through the . . . What did you say?' Mason turned from the door.

'I said, are you sure the back door is locked?'

'Yes. Now, come on.'

They went out, Mason pulling the door behind them.

It was snowing, steady large flakes thistledowning in the windless cold. Three or four inches looked to have piled up.

'You might have cleared a path,' remarked Jane.

'Sorry,' replied Mason. 'I didn't think it was this bad.' He opened the car doors, took the brush kept for the purpose, and went round the car sweeping the snow off the windows. Jane was right, he thought. He should have cleared the path. He grimaced as he felt snow fall into the tops of his shoes.

As they reversed out of the driveway, the snow crunched under the wheels. 'I hope this isn't too foolish,' he muttered.

'Nonsense,' replied Jane briskly. 'We always go to this service.'

'Tradition!' sang Mason, lifting his hands from the wheel to gesture like Topol in *Fiddler on the Roof*.

'Do be careful,' said Jane. 'We haven't had a white Christmas for years. Let's not do anything to spoil it.'

Mason sighed. 'It's more likely that going out in this will spoil it. D'you fancy a walk home if the gritters haven't got this far out by the time we're coming home?'

'I think that'd be rather nice. We haven't been out in the snow like that for years.' She laughed gently.

Mason grinned. He knew the picture in her mind—the two of them, hand in hand in the snow, over in the Old Town, one night, now years ago. 'We haven't had a white Christmas for years, either,' he commented.

'I've missed it,' she replied.

2

The church was filling. The organist was constructing a braid of Christmas music, and doing it well. Up in the gallery Mason hunched himself into his coat. Having the front doors open wide was no doubt very welcoming, but the amount of heat escaping must be enormous, and every time the inner doors opened there was a gust of cold air.

He leaned forward to watch the gathering congregation, as he usually did. This was the one time in the year that Jane could persuade him into a church, and they had come to this particular church every Christmas Eve for years. As Jane had said, it was part of their Tradition. He wondered how many others were there in similar case. He smiled quietly as he caught sight of one or two known faces. Men and women who would not usually be seen in a church, but were frequently down at HQ were always present.

And yet this year their Tradition was broken. Unspoken between husband and wife was the missing of their son, Eric. He was in the US, sent by his firm. Unfeeling of them to do that—yet Mason had also recognized the excitement and pride in Eric's voice when he had phoned to explain.

Down below one redheaded figure bundled in a green coat seemed to feel Mason's eye, and turned and peered up. Then, to Mason's surprise a hand waved in his direction—was it in irony or friendship? He marvelled briefly that Alfie had got past the custodians at the door, and yet it was Christmas. It was the time for waifs and strays to come close to the warmth. He shook his head slightly as he thought that. It fitted the thinker too well.

The Minister came in and took his place at the back of the communion table. The night began. Familiar carols soothed away the cares of the year. Mason's thought circled round and hit him again. Maybe that was why he came? Every year, to bathe in the affirmation of renewal? And yet he rejected that thought. Every year he also felt the appeal of something more. There was a cohesion here among the congregation that he recognized from way back in his childhood, from Sunday School. Maybe someday he'd have time to think things through again. Maybe his youthful opinionated rejection had been too hasty. He grinned at himself, and turned the pages of the blue stencilled book, seeking for the words of 'God Rest Ye Merry, Gentlemen'.

He found it, and sang. Then his voice tailed off. A rangy figure was going down the centre aisle, seeking a seat. It got half way, decided there was no room, and went back and down the faraway side. It found a seat just behind one of the pendant lights that illuminated the area under the gallery. Some children moved up at their parents' insistence, to make room for the man.

Mason sighed, and forced himself to relax. There could be no mistake. It was Kevin Allan.

Mason found it difficult to concentrate after that. Seeing the man reawakened all his questions. What had that tall, saturnine frame to do with the death in the Winter Garden? He felt sure there was something, despite the man's denials. Maybe he had got it wrong. Maybe that was a murderer down there. And then he began to worry. Maybe pity was distorting his judgement. He knew this man's son was in the morgue, and he had not told the father. When do ends justify means? he thought. Did cracking a case justify silence?

The service proper began. The Minister welcomed them all, his bald head gleaming under the harsh light that had been installed since Mason was last there. More carols were sung with great good humour. The amateur choir that usually was there made their usual attempt to mask inexperience. This year it went not too badly, although Mason could make out less than half the words. Still, there were no false entries.

Between carols, two young men read appropriate passages from the Bible. There was another carol. All the time Mason's eyes flicked regularly back to Allan. What was that man doing there?

There came the final carol before midnight which they sang sitting down. 'Silent Night' was always magical. He tried to find the right harmony as the congregation lullabied its way through that favourite. Funny how everyone knows that one, he thought. During the last verse the Beadle, tucked away at the far end, behind the choir, switched off the lights in pairs until the lights of the twin Christmas trees at either side of the pulpit were the sole illumination.

The organist began again his intertwining of melodies until the hour arrived. Then came the bells. This year they sounded much better than usual. Indeed, Mason even thought that they might be real, and not the awful tape-recorded version that had been used for several years past—the hiss of the tape quite ruining the magic. There seemed to be a couple of figures behind the right-hand tree, and at least one unscripted clang before the striking sequence began.

There was a prayer, and then the lights came up. Mason glanced across. Allan was still there, his large frame towering above the children beside him.

The Minister was speaking, welcoming them to what was now Christmas Day. Mason listened, at first with half an ear. The gift of the son—Mason warmed to that, remembering the birth of his own son. But then his blood slowly froze. The Minister was speaking, as he usually did, of the significance of Christmas, and of the coming of the King of Glory in the Baby. They were invited to think of God's sending of his Son—and Mason easily transferred that to Eric, over in the States. How he missed him!

But then the Minister went on to link Christmas and Easter. 'For this Babe came to die on a Cross.'

Mason clenched his teeth. He made additional links. He knew the traditionalities. Why did this old man go over what he knew? All that was old hat—and incredible. And yet, when *do* ends justify means? he had already asked himself that night. The answer was no clearer.

Mason felt himself going tense.

He hunched forward and stared down at Allan. The light gleamed on Allan's face, who had his head back and was looking at it. He had been right—he had been proved right—in profile Mason might as well have been looking at Russell Allan. He shivered. Jane Mason knew something was wrong, and put her hand on his sleeve. He shrugged it off.

'For God so loved the world that he gave his only begotten Son . . .' There was something there—something that tied up. Maybe it did make sense.

And then it was 'Hark, the Herald Angels'.

For once Mason found himself singing the proper words, without reference to pharmaceutical products.

The service ended with the Benediction, and then, as every year, various members of the congregation were smiling and shaking hands. Mason waited impatiently as Jane, more polite than he, responded to every overture. He glanced down, but Allan had gone.

But Allan had not gone far.

When Jane and Mason got down to the vestibule, Allan was waiting. Mason and Jane were making their way along to the door, shaking each and every hand as it was offered. Mason was on auto-pilot.

Allan stepped from a corner. 'I saw you up there,' he said, with a jerk of his head.

'Merry Christmas,' Mason was appalled to hear himself say.

Allan looked at him. His mouth twisted. 'Did you hear that man in there?' he asked. 'God so loved the world?'

Mason waited. Suddenly, as Allan cocked his head and pursed his mouth, he knew what was coming.

'I've been catching up on the papers,' said the other. 'I think you've got my son in a drawer.'

CHAPTER 13

THURSDAY

1

Allan stepped back from the body of his son, nodded silently, and turned to Mason. 'We better talk,' he said.

2

Mason stood at his window. The snow blanketed the car park. Crawford, sitting to one side waiting while Shepherd read Allan's statement, heard him pom-pom his way into a tune. Suddenly he realized it might be 'Good King Wenceslas', but Mason became conscious of what he was doing and stopped.

Crawford studied his shoes. He wondered how Shepherd might react, having been called away from his own Christmas family celebrations.

His thoughts were well-grounded. Initially, Shepherd had resented Mason's phone-call, but now he recognized the overriding importance.

'Well,' said Shepherd at last, laying the sheets down on Mason's desk. 'Is it solid?'

Mason came back to his desk and sat down. 'I think so, he said heavily. 'It just so happened that Allan and I were at the same Christmas Eve service.'

Shepherd waited.

'The address was about the loss of a son.'

After a pause Shepherd stated, 'You hadn't told him about your suspicions as to his son.'

Mason shook his head. 'Seems Allan spent a chunk of Christmas Eve in the Public Library reading the newspapers. The son wasn't back at his home, and Allan put two and two together. His son was at home only intermittently. Naturally, I suppose. They had regular rows.'

'The *Gazette* did refer to the body possibly being that of an assistant,' ventured Crawford.

'Mm. So he admits they had rows.' Shepherd tapped the sheets of paper. 'I can understand that. To give up University studies to run around with Antoine—that'd get me going if any of my kids tried that.'

Mason nodded. 'But it doesn't help me much.'

Shepherd nodded in turn and sighed. 'No corroboration. Crown Office'd throw it straight back.'

'But we at last have Allan saying Webster and Antoine were linked, and that Webster had been, shall we say "vehement" about him. His demands for a better share were jeopardizing the working arrangements.'

Shepherd put his hand on his own pile of files. 'It certainly would fit with what I've got. Not that Webster's a major player in my investigation. But it would fit if he were involved.'

'It might explain his car,' commented Crawford.

Mason looked his question.

'You remember that Jaguar in the car park at the Winter Garden?'

'Yes.'

'It's Webster's. I found that out late Tuesday. It didn't seem all that important. I was going to tell you when I saw you,' Crawford went on.

Mason's mouth twisted, then he conceded, 'Fair enough. It's not all that obvious a point.' He turned to Shepherd. 'But it would seem relevant now. And there's another thing. Both your investigation and mine have turned up a reference to a "Silver". In my case it's a Stephen Silver. Webster's got silver hair.'

'Agreed,' said Shepherd slowly. 'That all fits. It's a bit early for me, but you can't hold back. Not on a murder investigation. I suppose the only thing you can do now is have Webster in and try to break him.'

Mason shrugged. 'That's how I read it. But I thought I'd have a word with you first. Obviously your inquiries and ours now tie in together as we thought. Allan says that Antoine was involved with contract finagling. That does establish the link.'

'But I've not been able to key together payments with anything from those bank-books,' replied Shepherd.

'Webster wasn't at the Winter Garden when the strangling happened,' offered Crawford. 'At least, that's what he said. There's something short from him in the file, seeing he's the top man there.'

Mason turned to him. 'And?'

'Shouldn't we be able to break that somewhere? Find someone who saw him there?'

Mason shook his head. 'Allan says he didn't see Webster there. And that's entirely probable. It'd be quite possible for someone to go down from the Administrator's office to the Tropical House, via the Cactus House, and not be seen from where Allan was working. Come to that, the rear wall of that house is so big that he'd not necessarily have seen into the car park. He says he heard a car, but has no idea what it was.' Mason shook his head. 'No. There's no help there.'

'That seems quite a strong point in Allan's favour,' Shepherd interjected. 'If he was trying to get Webster he'd be tempted to make something up.'

'It wouldn't work if Webster wasn't there, and had a provable alibi,' Mason noted.

Crawford got to his feet and moved about. Then he

stopped and pointed at Mason's desk. 'The phone company offers itemized billing. I was thinking of asking for it myself. Might they be able to tell us where the phone call came from for Antoine just before he vanished?'

Mason looked shrewdly at him, then nodded. 'Maybe we can at least track that phone call. That'd be a start. Even if it doesn't take us very far. But as for the other matter, Allan's son. There's nothing to go on with respect to Webster— or anyone else.' He stopped, then changed to determination. 'You're right, of course. We need to have something.'

'How about just letting Allan go?' asked Crawford. 'Let him tackle Webster.'

Shepherd smiled a cold smile. 'That's tempting. But it would be quite wrong to do that.'

'We've got no cause to hold Allan,' Crawford objected.

'Come on, lad,' Shepherd said heavily. 'If Allan's not objecting to staying downstairs, it'd be better to keep him for a little. Remember he already assaulted Webster!'

'For reasons he hasn't given. In fact he says that Webster went for him,' Crawford replied. He didn't like this questioning. He glanced at Mason. Why was he not taking things up on their mutual behalf?

'Did you ask why?' Shepherd continued, peering over his spectacles at Crawford.

'Of course,' Mason interrupted. 'Of course we asked. But the point is, Alec, that if Webster did kill Antoine, the probability is that he also did the Studio as a blind. And if so, he's responsible for young Allan's death. We can't let Allan go, for Webster's sake. We don't know what he might do. For any sake, think about it. He's done Army time in Northern Ireland. He's trained.'

'If that is the right of it, why didn't Allan go for him when he put two and two together? Why go to church instead?' objected Shepherd.

Mason shook his head. 'I don't know. But he did. And that's why I felt the only thing I could do was to bring him down here.' He smiled bleakly. 'Jane was less than pleased.'

'You've not been home yet?' Shepherd was surprised.

'Quite so,' replied Mason.

CHAPTER 14

FRIDAY

Crawford suppressed a yawn as he came back into the room he shared with two other officers. His own desk was to the left of the door, the more senior man, Dickson, having the wider desk immediately beside the window. The other occupant, Horsburgh, was on Christmas leave.

Lucky him, thought Crawford bleakly. He was not at all sure that the trade of the week in London was an adequate compensation for being on duty over the Christmas period.

'Like your photo,' remarked Dickson as Crawford took off his jacket preparatory to sitting down.

Crawford grinned. 'Good, isn't it?'

Dickson nodded. 'She's the new city reporter at the *Gazette*, isn't she? Someone said she's Harry Irwin's niece.'

'That's right. But she got the job on merit. She's London trained.' Crawford stopped himself. Maybe there was no case to answer.

'Aye,' replied Dickson drily, and Crawford realized his error. 'That'll be right. Still, she looks a lively piece of goods.'

Crawford half-glared at him, but the older man was unaffected. 'I had a look while you were out. Funny, I said to myself. Young fellow bringing in a photograph.'

Crawford sat down, and re-positioned the photo. 'I just got it,' he said. 'Seems rather good to me.'

'Lovely frame,' responded Dickson laconically.

Mason came in. Crawford thought he looked tense round the mouth. Something was worrying him, but he knew better than to ask. Maybe something was breaking, but he'd hear in due course. Mason nodded politely to Dickson and turned to speak to Crawford. 'Have you got the forensic report on the fire?'

'Here,' replied Crawford, digging the buff file from the pile on the corner of his desk. 'I've got something else to tell you. Hell!' As he pulled it out the file nudged the photo. Crawford grabbed the frame before it toppled to the floor, then held out the file to his superior. He put the picture face down on his desk.

Mason took the file and looked quizzically at Crawford. 'Only family men have photos on their desks—and not all of those.' He turned the frame over so he could see what it contained, then grinned broadly. 'That's good. That's very good!' He picked up the photo to look more carefully at it.

'It's one of Willie Sheffield's. He's entered it for a competition,' replied Crawford somewhat sheepishly, uncertain exactly what Mason meant by the drawling tone of his comment. 'So I arranged to get a copy, as compensation for not forbidding its use.'

Mason laughed. 'It's a marvellous shot. I'd give it a prize. Not for your expression, but just . . .' He pursed his lips. 'Human interest? he hazarded. He held the photo out at arm's length. 'The sheer contrast of her and all those gloomy physzogs.' He put the frame back on the desk. 'Where's it being entered? Is it something I should tell the PR Office about?'

Crawford shuddered at the thought. 'Hardly, Boss. Hardly. It's going in some national press photo competition, but please don't tell PR—not even if it wins.' He rearranged the photo on his desk. 'But I must say I like it. I was appalled when I first saw it, but it has its points. It grows on you.'

'Like fungus on a dead tree,' quipped Mason. 'How'd you get it? Did he give it to you?'

'I saw a copy and phoned him. Lucy thought I should see it before Willie did anything with it.'

'And you got it from Willie?' Mason's eyebrow rose. 'Nice.'

Crawford followed Mason's thought. 'Yes. I got it from Willie. But Lucy did show me a copy first. He'd given her one.'

'Ah!' Mason responded. 'I see.' Then he seemed to slip back to the serious Mason who had come in at first. 'Give me about quarter of an hour and then come through. I want to go over the fire again. It's been two weeks and we've got to report on the review. In the meantime check with British Telecom about that phone question. They told me they should have something by now.'

He left, but Crawford caught a chuckle from the corridor. He looked at the photo on his desk and wished he hadn't brought it in that morning. It had been an impulse. He had been sitting quietly at home late on Christmas Day when the bell had gone. Lucy was down at her Uncle Harry's for the day, and he was expecting no visitors.

It had been Willie Sheffield at the door, with a parcel. He wouldn't come in, but handed over the parcel with a wink. 'Compliments of the *Gazette*,' he had said, and left.

It was the photo.

He had looked at it that morning and on impulse thought it might look well on his desk. Now he picked it up and considered stuffing it in the drawer.

Then he remembered. Dickson had seen it on his desk, and had heard the conversation with Mason. A swift glance showed that Dickson was indeed keeping an interested eye on what he did. Crawford put the photo back on the desk, more or less where it had been, and reopened the file he was working on as if it was business as usual.

What was biting Mason? he wondered. Something had

disturbed him. Had something come adrift on the Antoine front?'

He decided to go for a coffee before seeing his boss.

Mason sat with the files.

He sat back, forcing thought. Maybe if he thought through one line, his subconscious might do a similar job on this new one.

The morgue had been difficult. Aggravated by it being Christmas Day. Kevin Allan had looked impassively at the body, and then identified it. Then there had been that statement, lucid but not terribly informative. The Webster line Allan had indicated was possible, but unformed. It was all very well to indicate that Webster was involved financially or otherwise with Antoine, and that there had been words between the two on other occasions. But more was needed. Try something else, and maybe the Webster line would come clear.

There was something trying to coalesce in his mind. He sighed. Maybe Webster had nothing to do with the death. Maybe the solution lay in the extra-curricular photographs Antoine had taken. Blackmail—though there had been no trace of that. Unless the bank-books . . . but those showed payments in and out, with no regularity, and sometimes quite small sums.

Possible. But there was nothing to go on. Webster's statement was clear and simple. He had not been at the Winter Garden on the fateful Friday.

'Absence of evidence is not evidence of absence.' Mason thought of a line his son had shown him once in a book on extra-terrestrial intelligence.

He moved his shoulder and groaned a little.

He looked up at Crawford's knock. As he came in, Mason could feel whatever it was his mind had come up with, dissolve and disappear.

Crawford looked his question as he sat down.

Mason tapped the files. 'Antoine was a photographer. His studio was burned.'

Crawford waited. He knew these sorts of exercises.

'Now it may just be that the firing of the studio is a red herring,' continued Mason after a pause. 'But there's too much photographic connection in all this. Perhaps the solution is tied up with photos, and has nothing to do with Antoine's other activities. Those photos Paget found? There's no lead from them. If only there were other photos around.'

He sat up. 'Still, you didn't come in here to listen to me rambling. What've you got?'

'British Telecom advises that the call to Antoine did come from the Council offices. Unfortunately, it being Christmas, we can't find out which phone on their network was used—assuming they have a modern system. It might be on their internal log, if they have the sort of system that keeps track.'

'Long shot, that,' sniffed Mason.

'I was thinking,' said Crawford slowly.

He paused. Mason was about to make a joke, but suppressed it and waited. His assistant was thinking on his feet, and was probably best left to fumble his way to whatever he was trying to get to. A flippant comment might blow the idea away, and he himself had so recently experienced the annoyance of an inchoate idea taking wing before coalescence.

'You know that photo on my desk,' said Crawford slowly.

'Yes.' Mason frowned.

'It's just a bit of the negative, you know. Lucy showed me the original and really it's just quite a small part, blown up.'

'So?'

'There's the problem of the Orangerie. I just wondered

if we might see anything interesting if we could get hold of all the wedding photos that were taken the day of the murder. I imagine there were people in ahead of Antoine, for they were late in the day, weren't they? There might be something in the background. Someone who might be recognized.'

Mason sat back slowly. 'Good idea. Good idea. I wonder.' He thought a moment. 'Yes. There'd be a few weddings probably using that scene, if it was anything like a normal day. We'd need to check with all the photography firms whether they had used the hothouses on that day, and get permission, preferably from the blushing couples, to have a look at all the material. But as for the Antoine matter . . . Pity.'

He got to his feet, rubbed his forehead and then turned to Crawford with barely suppressed excitement. 'Wait a minute! Wait a minute! I bet the bride's mother went off with the photos that were taken out to the Brightside Hotel. If that's right we should be able to get most of the photos, even if the negatives are lost. That ought to be possible.'

'That's right,' said Crawford, getting to his feet. 'The Baradi girl said Mrs Regan was going out on the assignment, and that she would usually bring in the Friday orders on the Monday. Even if the bride's mother hasn't got the photos, Mrs Regan would.'

Mason's hand went to the phone. 'I'll phone my wife and get Mrs Elliot's number. You track the Regan line.'

Crawford left.

CHAPTER 15

SATURDAY

Webster shook his head at Reginald Opie. 'I know what I'm doing,' he said.

Opie's lips thinned. 'You do not know what you're doing,' he said. 'I urge you—'

'Oh, go away,' replied Webster, burying his face in his hands. 'I've done enough harm.'

'In that case I withdraw my services,' replied Opie. 'You—' his glance swept round the impassive officers—'are witnesses that my former client has rejected my advice.'

Mason nodded, and signed to Crawford, who opened the door for the lawyer.

Webster picked up the enlargement again and held it in his right hand. He picked up the broader view in his left. He looked from the enlargement to the other, and back. He sighed deeply and put the photos back on the desk.

'Russell Allan was your nephew,' Mason said quietly. 'You got Kevin Allan a job with the Council because he was your brother-in-law. Your sister had cancer, and Allan was ill as well. Northern Ireland had damaged him. He needed a simple steady job. One that didn't need too much thought.'

Webster picked up the enlargement again and held it.

'Antoine was a link man in the Council fiddle. He was the banker or something like that. You phoned him when you saw him at the Winter Garden and told him to come round to the Tropical House. You put up the "House Closed" sign, so you'd not be interrupted. When he came through, you strangled him. But you couldn't risk removing the body. You put it out of sight behind the orchid tree. That night you bombed the Studio so it'd make us think Antoine's death had something to do with his private photography. Your brother-in-law had told you his son was involved with him.'

Webster crumpled the enlargement in his large hand.

Mason stepped forward. 'You said you weren't there. But the camera never lies.' He took the photograph from Webster and flattened it on the table. He put his finger on the figure in the enlargement. 'They say your nickname is the Silver Fox,' he said.

'I didn't know the boy was there,' said Webster suddenly. He clasped his hands and put them to his mouth. 'I didn't know Sarah's boy was there.'

His head went down.

'We argued. About the other matter—the money. I was due a bigger lump than he'd paid me. He said something about paying Russell. I lost my temper with the wee runt. He was so arrogant. So arrogant. I just lifted him and shook him. He tried to run, and I caught him by the scruff of the neck. The chain was in my hand.' He lifted his right hand in a twisting motion, then dropped it.

The officers stood, silent, then Mason spoke.

'You expect me to believe that?'

Webster looked at Mason, then at Crawford and Shepherd. 'Please yourself.'

'Why didn't you come back and remove the body?' asked Shepherd quietly.

'I was going to. That evening. Later. After the Studio.' Webster hesitated. His hands went to his face. 'I thought I saw Russell through the window, after . . . after . . .' He gulped, then carried on. 'I phoned the Fire Brigade. But Russell never came out. They didn't come in time. After that . . .' He looked mutely at Shepherd.

'Did you lose your temper with Allan?' asked Mason.

Webster nodded, then to Mason's surprise, smiled briefly. 'Yes,' he sighed. 'I went for him when he was stupid enough to come back. I put money through his letter-box that evening and a note telling him to go away. But he went to the hills—his beloved bloody hills. And then when he came back he came straight to me. He didn't realize.' His hand went to the bruise at the side of his face. 'Yes. I went for him when he appeared. But you don't tangle with Army men.'

He shrugged. 'After all I had only done what he wanted to.' He stopped. 'To Antoine, that is. Deep down.'

'At the expense of your only nephew.'

Webster's white mane of hair lifted as he stared briefly at Mason. Then his gaze dropped.